Key Masters

The Tyrannosaur Rebellion

by
Gary B. Maier

Strategic Book Publishing and Rights Co.

Book Design/Layout by Kalpart. Visit www.kalpart.com

Strategic Book Publishing and Rights Co.
12620 FM 1960, Suite A4-507
Houston TX 77065
www.sbpra.com

ISBN: 978-1-62516-403-2

Acknowledgement

I would like to thank my son Brian St. John whose phenomenal love for books since he was a child made him grow up to be an editor and bring his knowledge and expertise into my work with this novel. I could not have done it without his immeasurable support.

Prologue

The mumbling in the Great Hall grew silent as the gong sounded. The council members took their places along the wall.

"We have waited long enough," announced Sentra the white crane. "The dinosaurs are not coming."

All heads leaned to look over at the three empty places reserved for the dinosaurs since the beginning of time.

"This meeting will now begin," Sentra continued as she stroked her long beard. "Fellow council members, we must come to a decision. It seems that the rumors are true. The tyrannosaur rebels have taken over their council seats from the brontosaurs by force."

A murmuring crept around the hall. "We must pray," Sentra said, raising her voice over the din, "that the brontosaurs have not surrendered the key to their door."

"Are the brontosaurs still living?" asked Zahar of the wolves.

"I have heard no word from them," answered Sentra. "But, we must expect the worst."

"You must send emissaries to talk to the dinosaurs!" Shouted Barca the mackerel.

"You know that one cannot enter another's sanctuary without invitation," replied Sentra. "But, perhaps."

CRASH!

The massive wooden doors to the great hall flew open, sending animals scattering in panic. The entrance of the hall darkened as a brontosaur the size of three African elephants heaved through the portal, blood oozing from several wounds along its body and neck, and fell with a deafening thud on the rough wooden floor. Screams echoed around the hall.

"Bonds!" Sentra exclaimed, landing by his head. "What happened?"

Bonds looked up at Sentra with a large hazel eye. "The tyrannosaurs," he panted, breath ragged, "killed the other council members." Bonds coughed up blood. "They wanted the key to Earth," he continued.

"Who is leading the tyrannosaurs?" Sentra asked frantically. Bonds closed his eyes, breath labored.

"Bonds!" Sentra cried.

Bond's eye opened a sliver. "Thorn!" He managed to croak.

"Who has the key?" Sentra asked, stroking Bond's neck.

After a moment's breath, Bonds whispered, "I gave it to . . ." His voice trailed away.

"Bonds! Bonds! Who has the key?"

"It is too late, Sentra," Zahar of the wolves said, putting a paw on the crane's wing. "He is gone."

"Thorn!" Sentra spat. "This is disastrous."

Panic gathered up momentum as news of the tyrannosaurs made its way around the hall.

Sentra flew back to her podium and banged repeatedly on the gong. The council grew silent.

"My friends," she started, her wings held outstretched in a calming gesture. "As you can see, we are in need of the key masters' help."

"But they are not ready," exclaimed Darius of the wolves. "They are still too young," he continued. Others murmured in agreement.

"We do not have the luxury to wait for the key masters to come of age," continued Sentra. "They are the only ones who can get onto the sanctuary of the dinosaurs. What do you think will happen if the tyrannosaurs are able to open their door to Earth?"

Silence fell over the hall as Sentra's last words sank in.

"What if the key masters do not succeed?" asked Barca, nervously splashing in his pool.

"That is something we cannot consider," said Sentra ominously. "They are both our and the human's only hope. I have already sent travelers to bring the key masters here."

Chapter 1

"The enemy is in sight," Tuck whispered to himself. "Come on, just a little closer."

Tuck Schneider was hiding behind the snowdrift he had built just behind his front fence near his enemy's yard. It was winter break and he was glad for it. He couldn't wait for Middle School.

Tuck was rather tall for eleven. His deep blue eyes peered through his thick mane of brown hair. He was a born leader with a larger-than-average ego and he knew that he could tackle any task with ease, which made most of the other boys at school envious of his talents.

Then, four months ago, Sienne McCally moved in next door and, to Tuck's disgust, it became obvious that her intelligence and wit matched his own. The worst came when Sienne embarrassed Tuck during a World Geography debate at school, correctly stating that during the early 20th Century, Melbourne was only the *temporary* capital of Australia, while Canberra didn't become capital until 1927.

After that, it was war.

Sienne, a pretty girl with thick, red, curly hair and freckles along the bridge of her nose and under her light-green eyes, had tried many times to talk to Tuck, apparently wanting to have a civil friendship.

Tuck wanted no part of being friends with her. He would never forgive her for humiliating him in front of the class.

*   *   *

Sienne was walking up to her front gate. As she opened the gate, she noticed a pile of snow that just didn't look right out of the corner of her eye.

Tuck! The name pounced to the front of her brain. She dived quickly to her right, behind her little brother Herb's dump truck.

At that precise moment, Tuck leapt out of hiding. He yelled his best war yell and let go with a hailstorm of snowballs.

Thud! Thump! The snowballs exploded in puffs of white as they hit the side of the dump truck.

"Tuck, you slime!" Sienne yelped as a particularly well-aimed snowball knocked off her knitted cap. "You'll pay, you weasel!"

"Ha-ha!" Tuck cheered triumphantly, not letting up with the barrage. "You're going down this time, McCally!"

Sienne was fuming. She turned the dump truck towards Tuck, and, tilting up the dump end to protect her from the snowballs, started pushing it towards Tuck's snow pile. Picking up speed, she headed for the break in the fence where Tuck had built his snow bank. He had purposely built it there to get a good shot at Sienne. Now he realized that his "advantage" was starting to turn against him. He watched in horror as the large red truck came bearing down on his snow bank.

Ka-thump!

Tuck just managed to dive to the side as his snow bank came crashing down.

Uff! Was all Tuck managed to get out as he landed face-first in the snow.

Sienne stood over Tuck, red-faced and panting. "How much longer are you going to keep this up?" she demanded. "Why can't we be friends?"

Tuck stood up and brushed the snow out of his hair. "It will be a cold day in you-know-where before we become friends, McCally!" Tuck forced through his teeth.

He turned abruptly and headed for his front porch. Sienne's gaze followed him to his door. Then, shoulders slumped, she trudged to her own door.

High up in a pine tree, two magpies were watching the scene play out. Their eyes followed Sienne into her home.

Ceril turned to Sonki and said, "The High Council must have made a mistake."

"Let's just wait and see," replied Sonki, preening her tail feathers.

Chapter 2

Bones was wagging his tail excitedly as Tuck came through the door.

"Hey fella," Tuck said, dropping to his knees to scratch his beagle behind the ears. Bones plopped down and rolled onto his back so that Tuck could scratch his white belly.

"Yeah, you like that, don't you?" Tuck said, the Sienne incident practically forgotten.

"I saw you and Sienne having a play date," Tuck's sister, Mallie, said as she appeared in the hallway. Tuck looked up, yanked from his reverie. Mallie was sixteen and almost six feet tall. Her long black hair was parted with two ponytails, which gave her an impish look. She was wearing her green training outfit for her volleyball practice. Her dark brown eyes peered over her reading glasses that were, as always, down on the end of her nose. Tuck always wondered how they never fell off.

"You know," Mallie continued, "you need to apologize to Sienne for the way you've been behaving."

Tuck opened his mouth to object.

"Let me finish," Mallie interjected.

Tuck and Mallie had a pretty good brother-and-sister relationship. He admired her aggressive volleyball game. They both liked the same kind of movies, and always were a shoulder for each other after having a bad day.

"Sienne came over to talk to me yesterday."

"What!" Tuck exclaimed. "What did she . . .?" He cut himself off when he saw the look on Mallie's face. The look he had seen many times when he should listen and not talk. Bones was now pawing at Tuck's hand, as Tuck had stopped scratching when Mallie began talking to him.

"Sienne is pretty upset. She doesn't understand why you're treating her like this," she said. Mallie got down to her knees and joined in scratching Bones' belly. The dog moaned with pleasure.

"What's going on, Tuck?" She continued. "She seams like a nice girl. And if I know your taste, she's right up your alley."

Tuck felt the heat rising to his face. "Yeah, I know," he said, looking down at Bones so Mallie would not see him blushing. "Maybe I have taken this a bit too far. But, I would look like a fool at school if I were to apologize to her now," Tuck said, looking at Mallie.

"Since when do you care what anybody at school thinks?" Mallie said in a sarcastic tone.

Tuck smiled. "You're right," he said.

"Well duh-*uh,*" Mallie replied, smiling back.

"I'll go talk to her tomorrow," he said sheepishly.

"No," Mallie said, looking at Tuck with serious eyes. "You will go over there and talk to her now."

"But it can wait 'till tomorrow," Tuck said, his voice lacking all confidence.

Mallie just stared at him.

Tuck stood up, sighing dramatically. "Come on, Bones," he said. "Let's go for a walk."

Bones sprang to his feet, his white-tipped tail thumping a rhythm against Mallie's leg.

Chapter 3

"Halt!" The Pterodactyl sentry called.

The hooded figure lifted up its head. Large yellow eyes glowed from under the hood.

"Thorn is expecting me," it said in a deep voice.

"Wait here," the sentry hissed. He turned, a leathery wing brushing the hooded figure's arm, and called to another sentry. "Tell Thorn that he has a visitor."

The hooded figure watched the second sentry hop awkwardly up winding steps and into the darkness where the torchlight didn't reach. A silent minute passed before the sentry came back down.

"You may ascend," the sentry motioned with a wing, tiny razor-sharp claws glinting in the torchlight.

The hooded figure nodded and proceeded to the winding stairs. He bounded up the steep stairs effortlessly. Upon reaching the top, a huge chamber opened up before him. The floor and walls seem to be made of giant grey cobblestones. It was dark and damp. Although torches were mounted along the walls, they had little effect. This was not a problem for his animal eyes, though. At the end of the lair, he could see Thorn and four other tyrannosaurs feasting on what looked like a cow.

Thorn looked up and called to his guest. "Ahhh, my old friend, come join us, will you?"

The hooded figure walked over and stopped in front of the carcass. "It looks tempting, but I think I will pass," he said with barely-disguised disgust.

Tusker, one of the tyrannosaurs, lifted his head. Glistening flesh dangled from his front teeth. "Not good enough for you, wolf?" He snorted.

"I like my kill fresh and not seething with maggots," the wolf said, glaring defiantly at Tusker.

Tusker's eyes flashed as he made a lunge towards the wolf. The wolf jumped to one side, swiping the tyrannosaur with his paw just

13

below his left eye. Tusker roared as his eye started to water.

"That's enough!" Thorn yelled, head-butting Tusker in the neck.

Panting, Tusker caught his balance and took a couple of steps back. He was not about to take on Thorn, who at thirty feet was almost twice his size.

"Ka-Dilla, you need to teach your son to curb his anger," Thorn said, glancing at Ka-Dilla with a toothy smile. She blushed and looked away. Ka-Dilla had liked Thorn ever since she lost her partner in a fight with two stegosaurs not long ago.

"What news do you have for me?" Thorn asked the wolf.

"The High Council has sent for the key masters," he answered.

"Good," Thorn purred. "Our plan is following its path."

"One of the brontosaur council members made it to the gathering," the wolf continued.

"Yes, I know," Thorn said, eyeing Tusker and the other two tyrannosaurs, Mauler and Kontch. "*They* were supposed to bring one of them here, <u>alive</u>."

The three tyrannosaurs shuffled nervously out of the reach of Thorn's massive head. They knew what happened when one makes too many mistakes. Gronk had recently felt Thorn's wrath when he had blabbed about he and other tyrannosaurs' plans to overthrow the dinosaur council. Gronk's bones are now being used for a playpen for pterodactyl young.

"Did he happen to say who has the key to Earth?" Thorn asked hopefully.

"No," the wolf replied. "He passed before he could say the name."

Thorn paced about, deep in thought. "So, that means the head of the High Council also knows not of who possesses the key. Thorn abruptly turned to the wolf. "We must see that the key masters are brought here. That will force whoever has the key to reveal themselves. Stay close to that fool bird Sentra, and inform me as soon as the key masters are here."

"Of course," said the wolf. "And what of my fellow council members?"

Thorn bent low over the wolf. "You need not to worry about them or any others," Thorn said in a low, guttural tone. "They will be taken care of, and you will get your due reward."

The wolf grunted his approval, turned and left.

Chapter 4

Tuck pushed the buzzer with a shaky finger.

"Can someone get that?" Tuck heard through the door, his heartbeat picking up pace.

The door opened. Sienne's eyes froze on Tuck. They stood there looking at each other for what seemed forever, when Bones rushed through the open door past Sienne. The short leash jerked in Tucks hand and yanked him into Sienne. Tuck let go of the leash as his hands came up to grab Sienne's shoulders to break his fall. Sienne fell back into the hall dresser with Tuck's nose coming dangerously close to her nose. They stared at each other for a moment, before Tuck jumped back as if coming out of a trance.

"Uhhh ... sorry," he said.

"That's alright," Sienne said, straightening her pink sweater.

"What was that noise?" Sienne's mother asked, walking into the hallway.

"Sienne was kissing her boyfriend," came a small voice from the top of the stairs.

"Shut up, Herb!" Sienne yelled.

"There's no need for that, Sienne," said her mother. "And <u>you</u> get back and finish cleaning your room," she added, glaring up at Herb.

"Sienne has a boyfriend! Sienne has a boyfriend!" Herb chanted as he skipped into his room.

"So," Mrs. McCally began, looking over Tuck. "I don't believe we have been officially introduced."

"I'm sorry, Mom. This is Tuck Schneider from next door," Sienne said, looking at Tuck inquisitively.

"Nice to meet you, Tuck," Mrs. McCally said, offering her hand. "By the way," she queried, "Did I just see a dog run into the living room?"

"Oh, dang!" Tuck exclaimed, running past Mrs. McCally to the living room. "Bones! Here boy!" He called.

Sienne and her mother followed Tuck to the living room.

All three froze, mouths agape, as they saw Bones sitting on the couch, nose to nose with a large husky-colored rat. Bones' black and white tail was thumping wildly on the couch as the rat's whiskers vibrated excitedly.

"Have you ever seen anything like this before?" Mrs. McCally whispered in amazement.

"It's like they know each other," Sienne said in a hushed voice.

"Well, I have to finish up in the kitchen," Mrs. McCally said, walking off. "And get those two off my leather couch."

Sienne and Tuck approached the couch and were promptly greeted with growls and snarls.

Sienne and Tuck hastily withdrew their hands and stepped back in unison.

"Alright. This is weird," Sienne said.

"You're not wrong," Tuck added.

Bones and the rat jumped off the couch together and ran down the hall into a room on the left, Bone's leash dragging along behind him.

"They're in the den," Sienne announced. "Let's leave them be."

"I'm, umm, a bit surprised at seeing you here," she said, looking at Tuck.

Tuck was still peering down the hall where Bones and the rat had disappeared.

"I seem to have been a bit of a jerk, lately," he said finally, turning to Sienne. "I'm not usually like that."

Sienne flashed him a look of, "yeah, right!"

"Would you like me to leave?" He asked, reading her expression.

"No," she replied. "This is the first time you've actually been civil with me. I have to take advantage of that."

"Well, I guess I'm at your mercy, then," he said, nonplused.

"Well, seeing that you are a boy," Sienne began, "I don't expect it to be easy for you to apologize." She put her hand up as Tuck opened his mouth.

She continued. "One little apology is not going to do it, anyway, for the way you have acted towards me since I moved here. So, I think it's best we call a truce and see how you behave down the road."

Tuck made a motion to say something.

Sienne stepped in quickly towards Tuck, so close that he was not immediately able to focus.

"I think your sister, Mallie, is a really neat person," she said, an evil smile forming on her lips. She stepped back and put her hand out. "Truce?" She offered, her smile now friendly.

"Um, sure," he said, taking her hand, not quite sure what had just happened.

"Would you like some hot chocolate?" She offered as she walked towards the kitchen.

"Hot chocolate? Yes, please," he answered, slowly emerging from his daze.

"Marshmallows?" She asked, glancing over her shoulder as she walked to the kitchen.

"Sure," he answered.

Tuck sat down on the couch. A moment later, Sienne came back with a tray loaded with two cups of hot chocolate and a plate of cookies.

"My mom just took them out of the oven," she said, following Tuck's gaze.

"Looks good," he said, taking one of the cups and a cookie. "What's the name of your rat?" He asked, taking a bite of a cookie.

"Noelle," Sienne answered.

"Noelle?" He echoed.

"Yes – " She replied, staring at Tuck. "Something wrong with that name?"

"No, not at all," he began, taking another bite of the cookie. "How did you come up with it?"

"She told me," she said, straight-faced.

Tuck spluttered, almost choking on a mouthful of cookie.

"Are you alright?" Sienne asked, patting him firmly on his back.

"Fine," Tuck said in a raspy voice. He gulped what was left in his mouth.

Tuck put his cup and cookie on the tray, not daring to put anything else in his mouth. "So, you're telling me that your rat can talk and it told you its name?" He asked in disbelief.

Gary B. Maier

Sienne took a sip from her hot chocolate, put the cup down, and turned calmly to Tuck. "Why so surprised? Don't _you_ have a rat that talks?"

"Why should I be in the possession of a _talking rat?_" He sputtered.

"Because, Noelle said that her friend Prodie was at your house and I ... _wait a minute!_" Sienne jumped up and ran down the hall into the room where Bones and Noelle were.

"Wait!" Tuck called after Sienne, as he followed her into the room.

Chapter 5

Sienne entered the room first. Bones and Noelle were in middle of the room, frolicking like a couple of puppies.

"Prodie?" She asked. Bones and Noelle both froze and looked up at Sienne.

"Yes?" Said Bones.

Sienne smiled as Tuck entered the room with a puzzled look.

"What's going on?" He asked, looking first at Sienne, and then down at the two animals on the floor.

The beagle rolled his eyes and murmured to Noelle, "If he calls me 'Bones' one more time, I will bite him in the kneecap."

"Now, now," replied Noelle. "He is only a human." Noelle scampered over to Tuck and, looking up with her big golden eyes, said, "It is nice to finally meet you, Tuck." Noelle's white body was flecked with dark grey markings with a long, dark streak running from between her eyes to her pink nose. Tuck shot Sienne an uneasy look.

Sienne nodded her head as if to say, "It's okay."

Tuck dropped to his knees and looked into Noelle's glowing eyes. "Umm, hi," he said. "It's nice to meet you, too." The tiny, outstretched paw grasped the offered index finger.

Noelle motioned for Prodie to come over. "This is my best friend, Prodie," the rat announced. Prodie plopped down next to Noelle.

Tuck stared at Prodie as if seeing him for the first time.

"What is the matter?" Asked Prodie. He tilted his white and brown head to one side, grinning toothily. His soft brown ears were arched inquisitively. "Cat got your tongue?"

"Why haven't you ever talked to me before?" Tuck asked, feeling a little hurt.

"Because you have been an immature bone-head ever since I came to your house!" Prodie bellowed.

"Prodie!" Noelle protested, embarrassed.

Sienne, leaning against the doorframe, folded her arms and smiled.

"Well, he *has*," Prodie continued. "You have not had to put up with him these past five months. I even had a note tied to my collar saying that my name was 'Prodie' when he first found me at his door, but *nooooo*... HE has to call me 'Bones.' Do not get me wrong," he turned to Tuck. "I *have* enjoyed my walks and scratches and attention, but when I saw what you were doing to Sienne – for reasons I guess I would have to be human first to even be able to fathom – the depth of the stupidity on your part! At first, I thought we would be seeing each other all the time," he said, turning back to Noelle. "But, *nooooo,*" he continued, looking back at Tuck. "HE has to keep up with his childish frivolities. I would not have taken on this job if I knew it was going to be like ..."

"Wait a minute!" Tuck loudly interjected. *"What job?"*

Sienne dropped to her knees and eyed Noelle sternly. "What's going on, Noelle?"

"Oops," said Prodie, looking at the floor as Noelle glared at him.

Noelle sighed. "I think the two of you need to sit down. We had planned to tell you under more calm conditions," Noelle continued, her gaze lingering briefly on Prodie.

"Tell us what?" Tuck asked, still looking hurt.

"Please, Tuck." Noelle intoned, motioning for them both to sit down on the floor.

*   *   *

"It is not our place to tell you all," Noelle began. "We have been out of touch with the High Council for the past five months."

"High Council, what High Council?" Questioned Tuck.

Noelle looked at Tuck with pleading eyes. "Tuck," she started, "I need for you to just listen to us. You can ask questions after." Noelle took a deep breath. "Prodie and I have been sent to be your guardians." Tuck and Sienne gave each other puzzled looks.

"Prodie did not just happen to appear at your house by chance. He *did* have to use all his puppy charm, though, when you first opened the door." Prodie made big sad chocolate eyes and gave his best look of innocence, when he saw that all eyes were now upon him. Sienne giggled.

"A miracle happened when Sienne moved here – which we thought would make our job easier bringing you two together. We did not expect this . . . ahhh . . ." She paused, looking at Tuck.

"Oafish behavior?" Prodie offered.

Noelle shot Prodie a stern look.

"What? You seemed to be having a problem finding the right words," Prodie said defensibly.

"May I continue?" Noelle asked.

"The floor is all yours, my queen," Prodie said, bowing ceremoniously.

"Mmmm," Noelle said, turning back to Sienne and Tuck.

"Sienne, I snuck into your school bag as you were waiting for the bus. I got the sense that we would click immediately."

"Well," Sienne began, "I *was* a bit shocked when you crawled out of my bag and onto my desk while I was doing my homework. Especially when you started to talk to me."

"I am sorry that I had to keep you in the dark these past months," Noelle continued, "I was waiting for Prodie to give the sign that it was time."

Prodie opened his mouth to say something. He froze in mid gape when Noelle flashed him a "just-try-it" look. Prodie, deflated, laid his head between his paws.

"Anyway," said Noelle, glancing again at Prodie. "As you know, a very long time ago, a huge meteor hit Earth. The impact and the resulting Long Winter caused many life forms to perish. There is a reason why man has found relatively few fossilized remains of dinosaurs over the years. This is due to the fact that for each group of life forms on Earth, like animals, mammals, reptiles and so forth, there is an inter-dimensional sanctuary where they can go to for safety. This is done by way of a gateway that opens when one wishes for it. Each group can only enter its own sanctuary. Prior to the meteor hitting Earth, the dinosaur pride was ruling here like savages and not obeying the laws laid down through eternity needed for a life of coexistence. It is said that the creator was upset at what was going on here on Earth and that he sent the meteor to teach a lesson. Many of the dinosaur pride returned to their sanctuary, but some also remained in defiance of the oncoming change. As we all know, most of the dinosaurs that remained on Earth did not survive.

We stayed on our sanctuaries for many years waiting for the Long Winter to pass. When we did finally come back, we had noticed that a new creature was roaming Earth – Man." Noelle paused for a moment and glanced up at the astonished looks on Sienne and Tuck's faces.

"The High Council," Noelle continued, "Which represents all life forms living in sanctuaries, had been watching Man for centuries and were astounded at the progress you made. The High Council then made a decision to give two humans, one male and one female, the gift of being key masters. Only the key masters have the ability to enter any sanctuary at will. The key masters are only needed when there is a crisis happening or about to happen that might jeopardize life on Earth. That brings us to where we are now." Noelle's eyes flicked from Sienne to Tuck. "You two are the chosen key masters for this era."

"So, what does this mean?" Tuck blurted out. "Is there some sort of crisis or something happening on your world?"

"Our homes are called 'sanctuaries,' not 'worlds,' Tuck." Noelle pointed out. "To answer your question, though, all our sanctuaries, to include Earth, are in danger. Well, to be honest, nothing has happened just yet, otherwise it would already be too late."

"So what *has* happened that you would need our help?" Sienne asked, crouching to look Noelle in the eyes.

Noelle cleared her throat.

"Well, you remember me mentioning the dinosaurs that left Earth before the meteor hit?"

"Yes," Sienne answered warily.

"Well, tyrannosaur rebels have overthrown the local council and are looking for ways to enter other sanctuaries – especially Earth."

"T-rex rebels!" Sniggered Tuck.

Prodie jumped up onto the desk, knocking papers and pens to the floor. Staring Tuck right in the face, he said in a sarcastic tone, "So, you think all those things you humans show on your moving pictures about dinosaurs rampaging through your cities would be *really fun* if the dinosaurs were real!"

Tuck blinked. "Well . . . ahhh . . . no," he said, leaning back out of reach of Prodie's flared teeth.

"Thought so," Prodie snorted. "Now, get this bloody leash off me."

Tuck cautiously removed the leash and collar.

"So, what is it that you think we can do, Noelle?" Sienne asked, still kneeling on the floor.

"That I can not yet say," Noelle began. "Sentra, the High Council head, will explain all these matters to you both.

"Where do we find this Sentra?" Tuck asked, glancing nervously at Prodie, who was now sitting on the desk, panting quietly.

"We do not have to," answered Noelle. "We will go to the bird sanctuary to meet with her."

"And where, precisely, would that be?" Tuck asked.

"Well," answered Noelle, "it is here . . . but not here."

Sienne and Tuck exchanged puzzled looks.

"I can not explain it any other way," Noelle said.

"When is this meeting supposed to take place?" Sienne asked, "I mean, we only have three more days of vacation before school starts again."

"We should leave as soon as possible." Noelle looked out the window. "You do not have to worry about time. I have already spotted the travelers in those trees nearby. They will take us to Sentra."

"Travelers?" Tuck questioned.

"Yes," Noelle said. "This is what we call those who travel between the sanctuaries and Earth. We are not birds, so we cannot travel to the Bird Sanctuary without physical invitation. Noelle turned to Prodie. "Prodie, will you check and see if Ceril and Sonki are still in the trees?"

Prodie trotted to the windowsill and peered out. "Yep," he said, "they are still there. They do not look too happy, either. Magpies are not too fond of the cold."

"Good," said Noelle. "I mean, good that they are still here, not because they are cold." Noelle quickly added, seeing Prodie's grin. Turning to Tuck, she said, "Tuck, would you open the window and call them in?"

Tuck opened the window and stuck his head out. There was a moment of silence, and then Tuck's head came back in. Tuck turned to see three pairs of eyes upon him.

"So what do I say? 'Come down here, birds?'"

23

Chapter 6

"Did he just look at us?" Ceril asked Sonki.

"I believe so," Sonki answered. "Not very talkative, is he?"

"Look at this, he is back," said Ceril.

"Umm – " Tuck called out, "Ceril . . . Sonki, could you please both come down here?"

Ceril and Sonki looked at each other. "I do believe he *is* talking to us," observed Ceril.

"Let us go see what he wants," replied Sonki.

In tandem, they dove off the branch and glided gracefully down to the windowsill. Tuck took a step back as the two magpies landed smoothly on the sill. They were impressive birds. They stood almost twelve inches tall, white and black splotches along their backs and wings. Sonki had dark red eyes while Ceril's were a deep black.

Sonki hopped down onto the desk. Ceril followed.

"Can you close the window, please?" Ceril said, ruffling his feathers, "It is really quite cold out there.

Tuck pulled the window down and moved closer to Sienne.

Sonki surveyed the scene. "So," she began, pointing her wing towards Sienne and Tuck. "Do they know what is going on?"

"They have been told as much as I can tell them." Noelle replied. "It is good to see you again, Sonki," she added.

"It has been awhile, has it not?" Sonki answered. "How is your little sister, Marielle?"

"She is well," Noelle said, "though I have not been in touch with our sanctuary for some months, now. I believe she was to go on a class excursion onto your sanctuary a couple of months ago."

"Indeed. I saw her there. She and her classmates were being shown around one of our nesting grounds by my cousin Floyd."

"Ah-hem!" Tuck said loudly.

Sonki and Noelle looked at Tuck. "Sorry," Noelle said, "I got carried away there. Sonki, Ceril, this is Sienne and Tuck."

Tuck and Sienne walked over to the desk and gently shook the magpies' extended right wings.

"Nice to meet you both," said Sienne.

"Yes, nice to meet you," Tuck said, his eyes dancing from Ceril to Sonki.

"Like-wise, I hope," replied Ceril.

Sonki nodded at Tuck and Sienne, her beak bobbing up and down. "We have been watching the both of you for some time now. We did expect this meeting to happen a bit sooner than now, though."

Tuck felt Sonki's dark red eye fall upon him, and he quickly looked down and pretended to be looking for something in his pocket. Prodie, watching the scene play out, snorted derisively.

"Alright!" Tuck blurted out, "I know that you all don't approve with how things are going with us – well, with *me,*" he quickly added, noticing that Prodie and Ceril were each about to make a comment.

"Can't we all start with a clean slate?" He pleaded with outstretched hands. "I mean, this is *a lot* of information for us to digest. It all sounds dubious. Don't get me wrong – I, ah . . . *we* believe you," he said. "I mean, how else would we all be here talking to each other if all this weren't true . . . right?" He finished, looking at Sienne for help.

"Tuck's right," Sienne offered. "You *are* trying to tell us that we are the only hope for saving Earth and your, um, sanctuaries from T-rex rebels."

There was a moment of silence as Sienne saw all eyes fixed on her. "I mean, what is it that you all expect us to do to stop these dinosaur rebels?"

The birds, rat and dog all regarded each other for a few moments. "We must see Sentra," Noelle finally said, breaking the silence. "Sentra will be able to answer all of your questions."

Chapter 7

"Okay," announced Tuck. "Let's go. Where do we find this 'gateway?'"

"It is right here," Sonki said, spreading one wing dramatically before them.

"What do you mean, 'right here?'" Tuck asked, a confused look on his face.

Sonki rolled her eyes, which didn't come across as such, her eyes being dark red against red and all.

"Well," Noelle started to explain, "remember, I told you one can open a gateway to their sanctuary whenever and wherever they need one."

"But – " Tuck started.

"Let Noelle finish, Tuck," Sienne hissed, elbowing him lightly in the ribs.

"Boy, I wish I were placed at Sienne's house, I like her!" Prodie teased.

Ceril released a little magpie cackle. "Good one, Prodie." Ceril and Prodie gave each other a rather bizarre inter-species high-five. Tuck's face turned red for the umpteenth time that day. Noelle looked up at Tuck with warm eyes. "Do not let them get to you, Tuck," she said, stretching up to his knee. "Once they appreciate the seriousness of what is happening, they will come around. They may not look like it," she looked first at Prodie and Ceril, then back at Tuck, "but they are the best you can have on your side when things start getting ugly."

Prodie and Ceril were doing a little ring-a-rosie dance on the desk. Sonki just stood there, slowly shaking her head in disbelief.

"Can you two knock it off for a minute?" Noelle said, her tone annoyed.

"Um, sorry," said Prodie. "We will behave now."

Ceril ruffled his feathers and settled himself. "Serious face . . . now *on*," he said with conviction.

26

"Sonki and Ceril are the only ones here with us who can open the door to bird sanctuary," Noelle said. "The rest of us need to maintain physical contact with each other as well as the one opening the door – or else, someone will get left behind."

Sonki hopped down onto the floor. "Hold my wings," she said, spreading her impressive three-foot wingspan. "Everyone else hold on and form a chain."

Prodie and Ceril jumped down and each took one of Sonki's outstretched wings. Noelle grabbed Prodie's quivering tail. Sienne and Tuck held hands while Sienne knelt down and held onto Noelle's pink tail.

"All ready?" Sonki asked.

"Yes," answered Noelle, looking around to make sure that Tuck and Sienne were connected.

Sonki closed her eyes and said in a dreamy voice, "Home."

A small shadowy hole opened up in front of them and grew rapidly in size. Sienne gasped as the hole ballooned, almost touching the ceiling. It was milky in color, as if full of fog. It hovered in place, barely touching the floor. Tuck and Sienne's jaws both dropped as the fog slowly parted and a thick green jungle presented itself right there in the room.

Sonki and Ceril wasted no time hopping through the gateway, with Prodie, Noelle, Sienne and Tuck being tugged through.

"Wow!" Tuck exclaimed, looking around at all the birds flying about. There were big birds, small birds, and colorful birds – but, most of all, <u>loud</u> birds. The chatter was nearly deafening.

Tuck looked behind him. "Hey! Where's the gateway?" He exclaimed, groping the space where they had just come through.

Sonki glanced around. "There was never a gateway there," she said. "To the inhabitants here, it just looks like we appeared out of thin air. No need to worry – nobody pays any attention. It is a daily occurrence here."

"Do you have to know exactly where you want to be when coming 'home,'" Sienne asked. "I mean, are there ever any accidents?"

"No, accidents never happen," Sonki smiled, which is hard to do with a beak. "You just have to focus on where you want to be. This ability is born unto every inhabitant in every sanctuary. They are only allowed to enter their own sanctuary. It is impossible for an inhabitant of one sanctuary to enter another sanctuary alone. You will always be placed where you will not interfere with any of the daily activities, or hurt yourself."

Sonki turned back to the front. "Follow me," she said, leading the motley crew on a path disappearing into the jungle.

Chapter 8

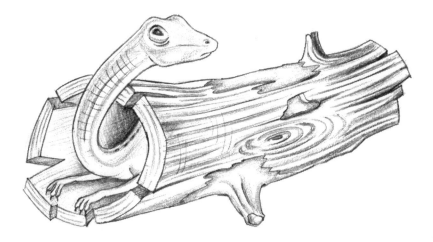

Panting, Yiddah dove into a hollow log lying under the thick low hanging brush. He lay perfectly still, forcing his ragged breathing to slow down.

The crashing that followed him came closer and suddenly stopped near his log. It was silent for a moment. Yiddah's heart pounded against his chest. He put his small-clawed hands over his heart, afraid that they would hear it beating.

"Did you see which way he went?" Came a rasping voice that seemed to come from the treetops.

"No," said a second voice. "He could not have gotten far, though." Tusker narrowed his eyes as he scanned the area.

"Well, our pterodactyl informant seems to have been telling the truth. It *must* have been this little compsognathus that he saw with that council member. I know his markings. I cannot remember the name, though. Never mind, I know where his kind hangs out."

"At least we have some good news to report to Thorn," Kontch said, obviously relieved.

"He will not be too happy that we let him get away, though," Tusker replied, still surveying the area.

"If we catch this little lizard, maybe we will not have to wait for the key masters to arrive to open the door to Earth," Kontch grumbled.

"Quiet, you fool!" Tusker shouted at Kontch. "He may still be in the area. No need for him to know how important the key is that he is carrying."

Yiddah's ears were already perked.

"Let us go back to the den," Tusker announced. "We can get some members together and go visit the lizard's clan before he has a chance to get in contact with the bird council."

Yiddah watched through the opening in the log as a huge, muscular and clawed leg passed by. He remained perfectly still until he heard the birds in the trees singing again. He then crawled soundlessly out of the log. Standing up to his full height of eleven and one-quarter inches, he glared in the direction where the tyrannosaurs disappeared.

"Who do you great, bumbling grommets think you are, calling me a *lizard?* Come back here, and I will rip your toenails off!" Yiddah spat. He then cocked his head to one side, listening intently, making sure that there were no sounds coming back towards him.

"Yeah, I *thought* so," he huffed, puffing his brown hairy chest out. The conversation between the two tyrannosaurs tumbled though his head. "What does this all mean?" He asked himself. "Why did that brontosaur have to give me this key?"

Yiddah opened his clawed hand, and stared in wonder at the shinny blue and green disc. "All he said was *'RUN,'* and disappeared. And now, I am being chased by tyrannosaurs!"

He turned towards the direction opposite where the tyrannosaurus headed. "I need to get to bird sanctuary and hand this over to Sentra. How do I get onto bird sanctuary, though? This is *not* making my situation any better. But first, I have to warn the clan that the tyrannosaurs are coming to raid our home!" In a flash of brown, Yiddah disappeared into the undergrowth.

Chapter 9

The motley crew exited the dark woods. Their eyes narrowed to slits as the sudden brightness hit them.

"It's good to be out of the woods," Tuck murmured.

"That is funny," Noelle smiled.

"No. I meant that I couldn't hear myself think back there with all that chatter," Tuck quickly added as he realized what he'd said. Then, he stopped in his tracks.

"Oh, my," Sienne whispered.

"No way!" Exclaimed Tuck.

A massive domed structure loomed up before them.

"What is this made of?" Sienne asked.

"Petrified wood. This was constructed a long time age. I mean, a *really* long time ago," Sonki said, following Sienne and Tuck's gaze to the top.

"In old times, when the creator walked with our ancestors, these buildings were built, one in each sanctuary. Of course, no two look alike. This one is made from ancient trees and branches woven very tightly together. Even when it rains, no water gets through. There is only one huge door at the front so that council members from other sanctuaries can meet when council gatherings are held. There are small windows scattered around the building near the top for birds in the audience to watch the proceedings."

"Wow!" Tuck said, "It must be at least fifty feet high."

"I think you could compare it to your capitol building in the city you call 'Washington,'" replied Sonki. "They are about the same size."

"You really have been watching us very closely," Sienne commented.

"Ah, well, we have been observing human progress these past 100 years with amazement at what you have accomplished, but also with a hint of fear at how you are also destroying the environment you live in. Sanctuary dwellers have seen the Earth destroyed once

31

before. We have a place to go to when things go bad on Earth. Unfortunately, you humans do not," Sonki said, gazing at Sienne and Tuck with concern in her eyes.

"Here comes Sentra," Prodie called out as a large white crane landed in front of them. She elegantly folded in her eight-foot wingspan.

"Finally," she said, looking from Tuck to Sienne.

Sentra was easily Tuck's height. Her long beard almost touched the ground.

"It is good that you all made it back safely," Sentra said, nodding at each in turn.

"It is good to be back," Sonki replied. "It has been too long."

"Sentra, let me introduce you to the key masters," Sonki intoned, raising a wing and motioning Sienne and Tuck to come forward. "This is Tuck and Sienne."

Sentra smiled at them both, her yellow eyes gleaming. "We have been waiting for you for a long time," she said, her voice warm and calming. Her long grey beak clattered as she spoke. "I hope your journey has not been too, um, shall we say, *mind-boggling.*" She smiled again.

"Well, we did hit a few minor bumps," said Prodie. "But, we managed to get past them," he quickly added, noticing Noelle's glare.

"It is an honor to finally meet you, Sentra," Sienne intoned. "We have been told an amazing story."

Tuck cleared his throat. All eyes turned towards him. "I wish to formally apologize for the delay of our arrival. I know that it is because of my – ahhh – immature actions."

"Tuck, Tuck," Sentra interrupted, putting a wing upon his shoulder. "You do not have to apologize for anything. It is I who has to apologize to the both of you for interrupting your lives. In our desperation, we have called upon you, and before you are ready to fully understand the responsibilities and powers bestowed upon you as key masters. I know that you have many questions," she quickly continued, as she saw the looks on their faces. "Let us go inside and I will provide the answers."

Chapter 10

The sunlight reached down from the small windows like long pale-yellow fingers, making oval designs on the densely trodden tree root-covered floor.

"Ooowwww!" howled Prodie. "Ooowww ... ooowww," came the echoes bouncing around the cathedral-like walls.

"Sorry," said Prodie, noticing that all eyes were now upon him. "I just have to do that whenever I come here. The council den on our sanctuary is not built to allow such great echoes."

"That is because you hounds would all be howling the whole day instead of taking care of business," Noelle said with a smile. The laughter from the group reverberated around the great hall.

"Shhh!" Sentra hissed. "Nobody move!"

"What's wrong?" Sienne whispered.

Sentra put one wing close to her beak. "Listen," she said.

Everyone strained to hear. Light tapping sounds seemed to be coming from the floor around their feet. Tuck looked down to see a huge rust-colored ant wearing what looked like tiny metal shoes, creating a sound not unlike someone drumming their fingers against a table-top as it walked along a petrified root. Although still diminutive, the ant was the largest Tuck had ever seen, almost as large as a king-size Snickers bar. The insect's serrated mandibles certainly looked down to business.

"Dang!" He exclaimed, taking one careful step back.

"Adam!" Exclaimed Sentra. "What are you doing here? You could have gotten yourself trodden upon walking amongst us like that."

A small squeaky noise came from the direction of the ant.

"We cannot hear you," Sentra said. "Use your voice enhancer."

Adam's middle set of legs fumbled with something green and cylindrical attached to his back. He put it to his mouth.

"Is that any better?" he asked, his high-pitched voice screeching with feedback.

Tuck and Sienne both jumped. Adam's twitching antennae turned in their direction as deep, red glowing pinpoints followed beneath large multi-faceted eye domes. "The key masters, I assume," his voice shrieked.

"Yes they are," Sentra answered, squinting uncomfortably. "Could you, perhaps, lower the volume just a bit?"

"My apologies," Adam said, gesturing demurely with his antennae as his second set of legs fiddled once again with the voice enhancer. "How is that?" He asked, his voice now emitting at a more comfortable level.

"Much better," Sentra said, visibly relieved. "Now, what are you doing here?"

Adam walked towards Tuck's sneakers, his six metal shoes tapping along in an even rhythm.

"How about you pick me up so that we could all be at eye level," he said, his hairy antennae feeling along Tuck's fraying shoelaces.

"Umm, ok," Tuck said, as he slowly laid the back of his right hand on the floor.

Adam stepped gingerly onto Tuck's hand.

"This feels weird," Tuck said, returning carefully to an upright position.

Sonki and Ceril flew onto Tuck's shoulders while Noelle scrambled up Sienne's pant leg. Sienne bent her elbow so that Noelle could settle on her arm.

"Hey!" Prodie protested with a pathetic snort. "What about me?" His eyes looked pleadingly from Tuck to Sienne.

Tuck stepped over to Sienne, holding out his hand with Adam, "Can you take Adam? Then, I could pick up Prodie."

Prodie's jaw nearly clattered to the floor in disbelief as Tuck carefully bent down so as not to upset Sonki and Ceril perched on his shoulders.

"Come on, you big baby," he said as he picked up Prodie and nestled him with both arms against his chest.

"Do *not* for a second think this makes up for all the trouble you have caused me – umm – us – well, maybe just a bit," mumbled Prodie with barely-hidden pleasure.

"Are we all . . . um . . . *settled,* now?" Sentra inquired.

34

"All good here," announced Prodie, his white legs dangling like pendulums.

Sentra leaned in closer to Adam. "What exactly happened?" She asked.

Adam stood on his four jet-black hind legs and addressed Sentra. "Your suspicions seem to be correct," Adam began. "It appears someone is working with the tyrannosaurs."

Sentra held up her wing to silence the murmuring beginning amidst the group. Sentra nodded once and Adam continued.

"As you suggested, we sent our most trusted ant members – unbeknownst to their hosts of course – to the other Sanctuaries to make sure everything remains peaceful. We have loyalists on the dinosaur sanctuary observing the tyrannosaurs."

"Wait a minute," Tuck interrupted. "I thought no one could get onto another sanctuary without a physical invitation?"

Adam looked up at Tuck. "We have our methods. We send our loyalists to Earth where they then search for a dinosaur and latch on to its hide. Then, they simply wait for it to return to its sanctuary. So far, we have two loyalists on the dinosaur sanctuary. It is not doing us much good, though, because the dinosaurs cannot return to Earth without the key. Because of this, our loyalists cannot report back to us. We do not even know if they are still alive. Also, the crocodiles, the only remaining dinosaurs left on Earth, now seem to be all staying put. It is almost as if they are somehow in on the tyrannosaurs' quest to overthrow of the council."

Adam looked back at Sentra. "One of our loyalists on the canine sanctuary witnessed something very extraordinary. She saw a cloaked figure standing in a clearing in the woods and heard it say 'home.' As the gateway opened, she could see vegetation only found on the dinosaur sanctuary. As the hooded figure jumped through the hole, the cloak parted and she saw the hind leg of a grey wolf."

"B-but, that's impossible!" exclaimed Noelle. "No species can get onto another sanctuary just by voicing 'home,' can they?" Noelle asked, looking at Sentra.

Sentra paced, stoking her long beard. "We have no time to waste," she said, looking from Tuck to Sienne. "We must get you onto dinosaur sanctuary."

Chapter 11

"There they are," whispered Tusker. Kontch, Mauler and two young tyrannosaur twins named Thrill and Seeker peered over the ledge down at the camp of the compsognathus clan. A grey-speckled pterodactyl landed silently beside Tusker.

"Did you see the one with the green markings down there?" Tusker asked without moving.

"No," the pterodactyl answered in a gruff voice.

"Go back up and circle wide. I want that little lizard . . . ah, now I remember, his name is 'Yiddah.' This cheeky little bugger has been a pest in the past."

"Shall I go, now?" The pterodactyl asked.

"Wait a minute," Tusker ordered, scanning the camp. "There!" Tusker pointed with a small, clawed finger. "His family is the group on the left near the fallen trees. Watch for any movement coming from near that area. Go now. Call out if you see him."

Yiddah watched from his hiding spot nearby as the pterodactyl kicked off and started to circle above his immediate family.

"I have to get down there before they begin their attack," Yiddah thought to himself. He scratched nervously at his chin.

The clan of compis went about their day, oblivious to the danger lurking on the ledge directly above their camp. Yiddah continued watching as Tusker gave orders to the other tyrannosaurs and they spread out and around the camp.

"I want the little lizard's family *alive!*" Exclaimed Tusker, his nostrils flaring. "I do not want Thorn getting upset like the last time. Wait for my signal."

Worried looks flashed across the other tyrannosaurs' faces at the mention of "Thorn" and "upset" in the same sentence.

"You can eat the other ones, if you like," Tusker continued. "Make sure you swallow them whole, though. Their little legs could get stuck between your teeth when you bite down on them."

The tyrannosaurs moved out, crushing bushes and snapping dried branches as they took up their positions to strike.

Tusker swore quietly under his breath as he looked down at the camp. The compis seemed to be having too much fun playing around to hear the tyrannosaurs, though.

Sweat ran down Yiddah's forehead. "I have to think of something, and fast," he thought, his gaze darting from one crouching tyrannosaur to another.

"Oh, stuff it!" He shouted out loud. He tore out from the bushes and galloped straight down the incline yelling at the top of his voice.

"Hey! Hey!" He called, waving his little arms in the air. "RUUUNNN, the tyrannosaurs are coming!"

"Get him!" Tusker shouted to the pterodactyl circling above. "Stop the others!" He called to the other tyrannosaurs.

The tyrannosauruses charged down the slope. The members of the compi clan froze in mid play, staring at the shouting Yiddah. A roar from one of the tyrannosaur twins jarred them from their stupor. Compis started screaming and running in all directions. The pterodactyl swooped down at Yiddah, his talons ready to grasp the little compi.

Panting, Yiddah looked up just in time to see the pterodactyl bearing down on him. Just as the pterodactyl reached to grab him, the compi stumbled over a rock. As he fell flat on his beak, he heard the *shick* of Pterodactyl talons slicing through air. The pterodactyl wailed in frustration as it flapped its huge leathery wings to gain height in order to make another pass. Yiddah picked himself up, spat dirt, and continued running down the slope.

The tyrannosaurs were already there. He watched in horror as two of his clan-mates were gulped up by a young tyrannosaur. He felt a jolt of relief as his father and sister reached the thick underbrush and disappeared.

"But, where is Mother?" He thought, panting. He looked around in desperation. There! The tyrannosaur called Mauler had pinned his mother down with one huge claw. She was alive, but her feeble attempts to escape were futile.

Yiddah noticed the shadow of the pterodactyl pass over him. He looked up just in time to see it coming around for another attack. Yiddah turned to run towards the woods, but instead found himself staring at two huge, leathery-grey legs.

Gary B. Maier

"Got you, you slippery little lizard!" Smiled Tusker.

Yiddah did not wait to hear what else Tusker had to say. He simply bolted between Tusker's legs. Tusker roared, turning to chase after Yiddah. Yiddah did not stop running until he came to a wide, fast-running river. He forced his breathing to slow down enough to hear if anything was still following him. Nothing. The vegetation here was too thick for the tyrannosaur to follow. He collapsed to the ground and started to sob.

Chapter 12

"Sentra, I . . . um . . . we know," Sienne began, looking at Tuck. "That all this is getting very serious, but," she hesitated again, looking at everyone in the group. "We need to know more. You say that we possess some kind of power that can help us get on the dinosaur sanctuary. I also think that there is something bothering you with the information that Adam here brought us about the wolf getting onto the dinosaur sanctuary."

Sentra lowered her head and closed her eyes. For a moment, there was silence. "You are right, of course," she finally said, looking up at them. "Come, let us go to the tea room and I will tell you all I know and answer any of your questions."

"You have a *tea room?*" Asked Tuck, astonished.

"Who do you think introduced tea to the Chinese?" Sentra said, smiling with her eyes.

"I need to get back to my sanctuary," Adam piped through his voice enhancer. "I have to be there in case any new information comes in."

"Yes, of course," Sentra answered, nodding at Adam, still sitting on Sienne's hand.

"Young lady," Adam said, looking up at Sienne. "Could you kindly put me down?"

Sienne bent down and placed her hand on the floor.

Adam walked off. "I will be in touch," he said, not looking back. "Home," he said in a dreamy voice. A small hole opened up to reveal huge brown anthills with black, white and red ants scurrying about. He stepped through the gateway and disappeared.

"That sure is amazing," breathed Tuck. "I mean, that you can travel places just by thinking them. And here we humans are still putting around in cars," he said as they walked through a small archway into a circular room. The scent hit their noses like a thick invisible wall. Shelves made of tightly flecked roots lined the walls from top to bottom. On each shelf, there were bowls made of the same-flecked roots filled with all different kinds of tealeaves.

Sienne took in a deep breath. "This is so amazingly beautiful," she said, looking around the room.

"How does all the smell stay in this room?" Tuck asked, wrinkling his nose. "I didn't smell anything before entering here."

"This great hall is so constructed that all the windows and the hallway door allows air to continuously circulate throughout," Sentra said before taking a deep breathe. "This room has no windows. It has only a small opening at the top, like a pressure valve, so to speak. It lets air trickle out so that new air can trickle in through the doorway, so the air doesn't become stale. Air is continually being pushed into this room, maintaining a higher air pressure and, at the same time, not letting any moisture to enter, which would not be good for the tea leaves. So, what kind of tea would you like?"

Sienne walked over to the wall and sniffed some of the different leaves. Still resting on Sienne's arm, Noelle's whiskers wiggled as she sniffed at the lower shelves.

Ceril peered around Sienne's head to Sonki. "Eucalyptus?" he asked.

"Why not," Sonki answered. "I have not had tea for ages."

"Do you have meaty bone-flavored tea?" Inquired Prodie, still happily nestled in Tuck's arms.

"I am afraid not," Sentra answered. "How about a smooth watermelon tea?"

Prodie gave it some thought. "Sure," he said.

"Make that two," Tuck added. "I've never heard of watermelon tea before."

Prodie looked up at Tuck. "Hmmm, maybe he is not so bad after all," he thought to himself.

Sienne and Noelle chose a lily tea. Sentra put small-flecked bowls on a flecked table in the middle of the room. Using her beak, she delicately chose the requested tealeaves and carefully dropped them in the appropriate cups. She then lifted a lid in the center of the table. Steam rose from the opening.

Tuck leaned over and saw water below. "Hot water geyser?" he asked.

"Very good, Tuck," smiled Sentra. She picked up a flecked ladle in her beak, scooped some hot water, and proceeded to fill each bowl, not spilling a single drop.

Tuck watched the steam from the bowls rise to the small opening in the ceiling. "Ingenious!" he exclaimed.

Chapter 13

The group left the tearoom and stood outside the great hall. Sentra motioned the group over to some tree stumps in a clearing that had been arranged like a picnic setting. They made themselves comfortable. The sun was high and warm.

"Is it spring?" Sienne asked.

"Well," Sentra began, "It is sort of spring here all the time."

"I like this," Tuck said, peeling off his sweatshirt.

"You mean, there is no winter here?" Sienne questioned.

"Yes. I mean, yes, there is no winter here," answered Sentra, sipping her tea with loud *slurffs*. "The weather is fairly stable with only slight temperature changes. And yes, lots of birds travel here for the winter," she added, anticipating Sienne's next question. "There are not many places left on Earth for migrating birds to go to anymore, what with the human population spreading out in such great numbers. So, many of us come home and then travel back in the spring."

Prodie lapped tea from his bowl, not stopping until the bowl was empty. He put his paw in the bowl to stop it moving, making sure that he didn't miss anything. Finished, he sat on his rump, licking his chops. It was only then that he noticed that everyone was staring at him.

"What? Hey, it was good tea!"

"Obviously," Noelle said with a smile.

"So, Sentra," Sienne began, putting her empty bowl on the ground. "How were we chosen for this, should I say, adventure?"

Sentra looked at the thick woods. Above the treetops, birds were flying about in great numbers, chattering and going about their business. "You have been chosen through your bloodline," she said in a serious tone. "You are both descendants from the original key masters who had the powers bestowed upon them when the creator left our realm forever."

"You mean, our parents were key masters, too?" asked Tuck.

"No, key masters only evolve when things occur that could shift the balance of all life forms."

"So there have been other key masters before us?" Tuck asked.

"Yes, of course." Sentra said. "The last time was during your Middle Ages, or what is sometimes referred to as the Dark Ages. There was once a fierce rat clan on the rodent sanctuary that called themselves the 'Dark Swarm.'"

Noelle squirmed about uncomfortably at the mention of the Dark Swarm.

"Their leader, Nager, was a ruthless leader. The High Council at that time made the mistake of letting Nager rule over the rodent sanctuary, hoping that would make him happy and keep the peace. Nager had bigger plans, though. He sent millions of his clan members onto the European continent on Earth with the intention of decimating the human population."

"But why?" questioned Sienne. "What was he trying to gain?

"I guess one could say that he had a human trait in him. He wanted to control more land. He knew that the humans were weak and susceptible to disease. Much of the human population at that time was living in crowded and unsanitary conditions, which made it easy for Nager to spread his disease amongst them. As you know, millions of humans died during that time."

"Did the key masters manage to defeat the rats?" Tuck asked.

"Yes, but it was not easy. Sienne, your ancestors come from Ireland and Tuck, your ancestors are from Germany, but I'm sure that you both know that. We did have some language difficulties. The key masters at the time were in their late twenties. At that time in your history, the English and the Germans were not the best of friends, if you know what I mean. It was not easy getting them to work together. The powers of the key masters can only work if they are willing to work together. I am sure that many human lives would have been saved if the key masters had been able to work together from the very beginning."

"What were their names?" Sienne asked.

"Sorry?" Sentra said, taken aback at the question.

"The key masters," Sienne repeated. "What were their names?"

"Um, her name was Isabella Kinny, and . . . he was named Maurice Schneider," she said with a questioning look in her eyes.

"They had a child together, didn't they?"

"How did you . . . um, why do you say that?" Sentra asked, not able to hide the shock in her voice.

"So, it's true then, the stories that my grandmother told me when I was a little girl. She told me about her great-grandmother many times past – that she had a child that was supposedly sired by the son of a German Lord from the Royal House of Schneider. If this is the same Maurice Schneider – and it must be – then it was told that his father ran him out of the house when Maurice told him that he was in love with an Irish girl without nobility and that she was with his child. That's all I can remember being told," Sienne looked at Sentra. "Do you know what happened to them? Did they ever get back together?"

Sentra sighed as sadness enveloped her eyes. "No, they did not see each other ever again. It is told that Maurice traveled all over the English Islands looking for her. It was not easy with his German background. After many years, he finally settled down in a Scottish village and married and had four children. On many evenings, he was seen sitting in the fields gazing out for hours." She paused. "Isabella went back to her family, but was shunned by them when see told them about her love for Maurice. She left and went to Wales. She never married again but raised a beautiful daughter."

"Does that mean that we're related?" Tuck asked in disbelief looking from Sentra to Sienne.

No one answered.

"Okay, I can deal with that . . . I think," he said, shuffling uncomfortably. "Alright, what happened with the rats?" He asked, still looking unsettled with the news.

"Oh, yes," Sentra said, happy at the chance to change the subject. "Well, you now know that Isabella and Maurice . . . ahhh . . . finally came to an agreement."

"Well, duh!" exclaimed Tuck.

"Anyway," she continued, "together with the power of telepathic mind-control, they managed to hoard the rats into large groups and send them to a high-walled island on rodent sanctuary where they were tried by the high council and punished by the laws governing the rodent sanctuary."

"That's it?" exclaimed Tuck. "It was that easy?"

"Tuck," Noelle said, "It took almost five years to round them all up."

"Oh," he said.

"You don't know how hard it has been for us rats. For generations, no one has trusted us."

"What happened to Nager?" Tuck asked.

"Once he got wind of what happened to his clan on Earth, he fled with his family," Noelle explained. Throughout the times, there have been signs of his offspring, but any time one of his kind is seen, it is reported to the council. It has been almost sixty years since the last sighting. We all hope that they have died out or have bred with other clans."

Chapter 14

"So, I guess that means we have telepathic mind-control abilities," Tuck said, smiling.

"I hope you do not think that it will simplify things against a tyrannosaur," Sentra said. "Rats can be easily led, no offence meant," she added, glancing down at Noelle.

"None taken," Noelle said.

Sentra looked back at Tuck and Sienne. "Different situations will require different special powers. I do not yet know what powers you may have. It has been witnessed with different key masters that they never have the same powers. I only know that you are able to get onto any sanctuary you choose. So, Tuck, sorry to burst your mind-control powers bubble, but it may not be much use against a tyrannosaur."

Sienne patted Tuck on the shoulder. "That's okay, I'm sure we have some other cool powers," she smiled.

"Yeah, maybe you can conjure up juicy steaks at will," snorted Prodie. Curious looks came from the treetops at the laughter coming from the group in the clearing.

Sonki's voice cut through the laughter like a sharp knife. "You need to tell them about the wolf."

All fell silent at the sudden seriousness in Sonki's voice.

"Ah yes," Sentra said. "The wolf," she stroked her long beard in thought.

"What I am about tell you," she began, "is all speculation. It is told that a long time ago, a female wolf and a young male dinosaur fell in love and had young together. These wolf offspring apparently had the ability to cross back and forth to the dinosaur sanctuary without the physical presence of a dinosaur. A very intelligent wolf called Viejo formed a small band that wore dark capes with hoods. They never tried to take over the counsel or bully or rule anything. That is why no one can vouch for their existence. It is said that they worked closely with some of the dinosaurs that wished to rule on Earth throughout the ages. The story goes that these wolves went to the North American area you now call Alaska to clear land of humans to use as a home base to start raids with dinosaurs on the dense human settlements further south. At first, the wolves were doing very well. Humans were disappearing at an alarming rate. Then, the humans invented firearms and were able to ward off and kill these wolf packs. Since that time, I have not heard of a cloaked wolf sighting. Until now, that is."

"Do you believe these wolves exist?" Sienne asked.

Sentra stroked her beard and looked at Sonki.

"Yes we do," answered Sonki. "We have been trying for many years to find a trail to these wolves. We only come up with dead ends. If they are working with the tyrannosaurs, then that could make our work much more difficult and extremely dangerous," she said, looking from Tuck to Sienne with her dark eyes.

"So, what's the plan?" Tuck asked.

"We have to get you on the dinosaur sanctuary and find who has the key to the door to Earth before the tyrannosaurs get hold of it," Sentra answered.

"You don't know who has it?" Sienne asked.

"No. The last dinosaur council member passed away before he could tell us who he gave it to."

"That means the T-rex don't know who has it, either," said Tuck.

"That is what we are hoping, at least so far, anyway."

"What do you mean, 'so far?'" Sienne questioned.

"Well, if the tyrannosaurs had the key already, we would not be here drinking tea."

Tuck took a deep breath. "Okay, what do we need to do to get us on the dino sanctuary?"

"You and Sienne have to hold hands and say 'home dinosaur sanctuary' in a very calm voice."

"Well," Tuck started, "how do we know where we are going to end up? I mean – we don't want to pop out amongst a pack of T-rexes."

"Don't worry. You have the ability to choose where you enter. When one window opens up, if you do not like it, you can say, 'new site,' and a new window will open up for you. I suggest you choose somewhere high so that you can get a good view of your surroundings."

"You're not coming with us?" Sienne asked with a worried expression.

"I have to stay here in case other information comes to me from our sources on the different sanctuaries," Sentra explained, placing a wing on Sienne's shoulder. "You both will do just fine. Noelle, Prodie, Sonkie and Ceril will be with you the whole time. You are in good hands – well, paws and wings," she said, smiling at Sienne.

"Alright then," Tuck said in a brave voice. "Find the dino who has the key, defeat the T-rexes, and save Earth. Sounds easy enough."

"That is the spirit," announced Ceril. "No worries."

"Just remember," Sentra added, "Stick together. Without the connection of each other, Sonki and Ceril can only return here, and Prodie can only go to his sanctuary as Noelle only to hers."

Chapter 15

"Is she still alive?" Thorn asked, nonplussed. He picked at his stained teeth with a long sharp bone.

"Yes," answered Ka'dilla. "Barely, though. Her leg is badly broken. She will not eat anything and just stares at the wall."

"No matter if she dies. It is enough that they know that we have her." Thorn spat as he tossed the bone aside. "Are the others back yet?"

"No, my dear. They are still out looking for the compi."

"Bungling fools!" Thorn roared. "How could they have let him get away again?"

"Calm down, my sweet," Ka'dilla purred, rubbing her head along his neck. "No need to be so hard on them. Things are going as you planed. The key masters will be here soon, and we will have the key to Earth."

Thorn grunted as the footsteps of a large pterodactyl echoed off the walls.

"What is it?" Thorn asked.

"The wolf is here," the pterodactyl announced. "Shall I have him come up?"

"What does he want?" Thorn asked in annoyance.

The pterodactyl stood silently staring at Thorn.

"Very well," Thorn sighed. "Send him up."

The pterodactyl turned and labored down the steep stairway.

"If they were not able to fly," he said, watching as the winged beast disappeared down the stairs, "I would have no use for them."

The cloaked wolf came up the stairs, its yellow eyes glowing from under the hood.

"What do you have for me?" Thorn asked.

"Nice to see you, too," the wolf growled under its breath.

"What was that?" Thorn said, looking down at the wolf.

49

"My council members are becoming suspicious of my disappearances. I have rounded up 200 clan members for our cause. I will not be able to keep this quiet for much longer."

Thorn gave him an evil grin. "Wolf, you do not seem to have much confidence in our abilities."

"That . . . has crossed my mind," the wolf answered, matching Thorn's gaze.

Thorn's hearty laugh echoed throughout the chamber. "I like you, wolf. You are a feisty one." Thorn's smile faded quickly as he bent down closer to the wolf. "Do not make the mistake of underestimating me, wolf. The key masters are on their way. Everything is going as I planned," he looked back at Ka'dilla, pleased with himself.

"I am impressed," the wolf commented dryly.

"You just be ready to move," Thorn said, turning back to the wolf. "As soon as we have the key masters here, you need to open your gateway and let us into your sanctuary to take control of the rest of your council. Then, you can mobilize the rest of the clans for the first stage of the assault on Earth. You will of course make it clear that any inhabitant on your sanctuary that does not want to be a part of our cause will be killed."

"Of course," the wolf nodded. "I will, however, expect your invaders to leave my sanctuary once I have control of the council," he added.

A flash of anger crossed Thorn's face, which he quickly replaced with a toothy grin. "You have my word that we will retreat from your sanctuary as soon as the first phase has been completed. Now, leave me. You will be informed when we are ready for you," he said, turning his back to the wolf.

The wolf squinted his eyes in hatred, shot a glance at Ka'dilla, turned and left.

Chapter 16

"Are we all connected?" Tuck asked, looking back at the line of animals behind him. He smiled at the eyes that looked up at him. "This has to be the most amazing adventure that could happen to anyone," he thought, "and it's happening to *me.*"

"All looks good here," Sonki replied from the back of the line.

"Well, okay, then," Tuck said, taking a deep breath and turning to Sienne. "Are you ready?" He asked.

"As ready as I will ever be," she answered, grabbing Tuck's hand.

"On three, then."

"One, two, three, *home dinosaur sanctuary,*" they said in unison.

A fist-sized, shimmery hole opened up in the air a few feet in front them at about chest height, growing rapidly in size. Before either of them could react, an arid plain lay before them with dead and dying trees dotting the tundra. From the left, a tyrannosaur stomped into view. Tuck gasped while Sienne went frozen.

It turned slowly to look with one orange eye at the strange creatures apparently hovering in mid-air as though dangling from a large stick. It blinked. Overcoming its surprise, it roared.

Tuck and Sienne both screamed as the tyrannosaur came charging towards them. The bottom rim of the opening was too high for the rest of them to see what all the commotion was about.

"What is happening?" Ceril squawked, flapping his wings to get a look.

"New site!" Sienne yelled, squeezing Tucks hand. Nothing happened.

"Tuck!" She yelled again, pulling Tuck in front of her. "We have to say it together!"

The tyrannosaur loomed closer.

"New site!" They screamed together.

The gateway disappeared just as the tyrannosaur clamped his jaw over the hole.

Tuck and Sienne stumbled through the new opening with the others dragged along behind squawking, squeaking and howling, falling into a tangled heap.

"What was *that* all about?" Prodie asked, as he pulled himself out from under Ceril.

"You don't want to know," Tuck said meekly as he dusted of his shirt.

"Is everything alright, Sienne?" Noelle asked.

"Ahhh . . . that first option was definitely not a good start," Sienne said, her knees visibly shaking. "We may be in some trouble. A T-rex spotted us. I think we may have lost our element of surprise."

Everyone went quiet at the mention of the tyrannosaur.

"Let me see if we can get our bearings," Sonki said with renewed purpose, looking around.

They were standing atop a small sparsely covered green hill surrounded by brown prickly scrubs. The sun was high in the cloudless sky. Strange sounds were coming from the thick woods in the distance.

"Sure is humid here," Tuck breathed, wiping sweat from his brow.

"Sonki, do you know where we are?" Noelle asked.

Sonki pointed a wing into the direction of an outcropping of jagged mountains in the distance.

"That is where the dinosaur council is housed."

"So, that's where we have to head," Tuck said, kneeling beside Sonki. Sienne sat down with Noelle resting in her lap. Prodie lay down with his head resting on Tuck's knee. Tuck automatically started scratching him behind the ear. Ceril hopped onto Sienne's shoulder.

They all looked silently towards the menacing mountains in the distance.

Chapter 17

"They are here!" Kontch rasped breathlessly as he stumbled into the clearing.

"Who is here?" Mauler growled, displeased that his lunch of a young stegosaur was being interrupted.

Kontch raised a small claw to give himself a moment to catch his breath. He gulped once. "The key masters," he said. "I saw them materialize out on the dry plain."

Mauler and the twin tyrannosaurs, which were waiting for Mauler to finish eating so that they could get their turn, lumbered over and hovered over Kontch.

"Did you see anyone with them?" Mauler asked with excited eyes.

"No, I saw only the two humans, but they saw me and disappeared again before I could grab them."

"Damn it!" Spat Mauler. He started pacing.

"Should we tell Thorn?" Seeker asked nervously.

Mauler stopped pacing and looked from Seeker to the others.

"No, we will get the pterodactyls to search the area from the air. Telling Thorn that we saw the key masters, but not knowing where they are now, will not exactly put us in his favor."

The tyrannosaurs all grunted in agreement.

"Go to the pterodactyl's lair and have them circle the area," Mauler ordered the twins.

The twins turned and stomped off into the underbrush.

"And, make sure that they tell us as soon as they see any sign of them," he shouted after them.

"Come on," Mauler said to Kontch. "We have to keep looking for that bloody compi," he continued in a disgusted voice as his eyes fell momentarily onto his half-finished meal.

Chapter 18

The bright sun stood high in the sky as the motley crew labored through the dense brush. Tuck and Sienne swatted at large mosquito-like insects buzzing around their faces. Noelle nestled happily against Sienne's neck. Prodie trotted ahead of the group, easily navigating the low brush.

Sonki and Ceril were flying above them surveying the area for signs of danger.

"Yuck!" Exclaimed Tuck, looking down at the gooey smear on the front of his checkered shirt from the bug he just swatted. He looked up at the two magpies as he wiped his hand on his pants. "Hey, Sonki," he called.

Sonki glided down lower. "What is it?" She asked.

"Is there maybe a place up ahead to rest? The humidity and bugs are really wearing us out."

"Yes, somewhere with water, if possible," commented Sienne, her red curly hair matted against her face.

"There is a small stream up ahead about thirty minutes away," Sonki said. "I was planning for us to stop there, anyway."

Prodie's head protruded out of the underbrush, his tongue hanging out the side of his mouth. "What is the hold-up?" He said, panting heavily.

"We will be resting up soon," said Sienne. "Can you take Noelle for a bit? Her body is too hot on my neck."

"I am okay," said Noelle. "I can walk on my own for awhile."

"Are you sure?" Sienne said with concern. "I don't want anything trying to grab you."

"I will walk with her," Prodie said, smiling at Noelle. Noelle walked over to Prodie and rubbed her face against his neck.

"Hmmm," said Sienne, leaning over to Tuck. "Have you ever seen a beagle blush before?"

"All right then," Tuck began, his eyes lingering on the blushing

Prodie. "Let's get to that stream." He opened and closed his sticky hand with a look of disgust.

*　　*　　*

Reaching the stream, Tuck bent down to wash his hands and took off his shirt to wash out the bug stain that had started to crust and was attracting dark-blue flies with bright yellow wings. Prodie and Noelle were eagerly lapping water while Sonki and Ceril cut orbits above them, widely circling the area.

Tuck began to take off his shoes and socks and rolled up his pants.

He hesitated, looking up at Sonki and Ceril, who had settled on a low branch. "Do I need to worry about anything in this water that bites?"

Sonki looked up and down the stream. "I do not think so," she began. "This is very shallow and clear running water. No place for anything to hide."

"Watch out for leaches!" Ceril called out as Tuck put one foot in the water.

Tuck stumbled back and fell on his butt.

"Only joking," Ceril said, laughing.

"You're funny, you know that?" Tuck commented, lying on his back and smiling up at Ceril.

"Do I see a sense of humor arising from you?" Ceril questioned, as he glided down and gently landed on Tuck's stomach. Tuck squinted, an evil smile spreading over his face. Ceril noticed the smile spreading. The shock was visible in Ceril's eyes . . . but too late. Tuck grabbed the magpie before he could fly off, and jumped into the stream, dunking the squawking Ceril. On the bank, the others rolled around, laughing at the spluttering Ceril.

Tuck put Ceril on his knee as he sat in the water. The bird coughed and shook himself. Tuck's smile actually extended to both ears as he looked at Ceril. Ceril started to laugh, with Tuck joining in.

55

Chapter 19

The group settled under thick overhanging bushes near the bank of the stream.

Crickets played their loud rhythmic sonata as light from the midday sun danced on the running water. Sitting in the high branches, Sonki and Ceril had spread their wings in hope of catching a welcome breeze. Ceril's eyelids were fighting a losing battle with gravity. Prodie was panting heavily as Noelle slept at his side.

"I have never heard such loud crickets," Tuck commented.

Sienne lifted her head off Tuck's shoulder. "What?" She said in a sleepy voice.

"The crickets," he repeated. "I have never heard anything so loud."

"Mmmm," murmured Sienne, as she laid her head back onto Tuck's shoulder.

Sonki watched a pterodactyl carving large circles high above in the sky.

She dropped her gaze to the group below, making sure that they were all well hidden by the thick bushes. Content that they were safe, she fixed her gaze back to the pterodactyl again until it moved on.

Tuck looked over to Prodie only to see him staring at him. Tuck quickly looked away, but decided to look back into Prodie's dark staring eyes.

"Umm," Tuck began, "is everything okay?" He asked.

"Oh, sorry," Prodie said, now realizing that he was staring. "I have just been thinking about how much you have changed in this short time."

Tuck couldn't hide the look of surprise on his face.

"Do not get me wrong," Prodie said, reading Tuck's reaction. "It is all good. I just was not expecting this change in you."

"Umm – thanks, I guess," Tuck said, frowning. "A lot has happened. It still boggles my mind when I think about it. So what's the story with you and Noelle?" Tuck asked, quickly changing the subject as his eyes lingered on the sleeping rat.

Prodie looked down at Noelle, now curled up between his outstretched legs.

"We are both in the council on our respective sanctuaries," he said, giving Noelle an endearing lick on the head.

"We met at a gathering in the Great Hall on bird sanctuary some time back and became really close."

Prodie paused, pricking his ears.

"What is it?" Whispered Tuck looking about.

"Nothing," answered Prodie, relaxing his ears again. "Just a lizard, I guess."

"Anyway," he continued, "You know now that one can only return to their own sanctuary."

"Yes," Tuck answered.

"Well, council members from all the sanctuaries can also travel to the Great Hall when meetings are held. That is where we would meet. After the meeting, we would either go to Noelle's sanctuary or to mine and spend time together. When this rebellion on the dinosaur sanctuary seemed likely to happen, Sentra was asking for volunteers to guard the key masters. Once we found out that the key masters dwelled so close together, we volunteered immediately".

Tuck lowered his head in shame.

"Hey," Prodie said in a soothing tone.

Tuck raised his head, his eyes red.

"Forget about before," Prodie said, his eyes like big drops of chocolate. "Neither of us can change that. As much joking around that we do," he paused to take a deep breath. "This is not going to be easy. The tyrannosaurs are extremely violent and will do everything in their power to get the key to Earth. Most likely, they will also try to invade the other sanctuaries as well. We have to work together and we do not yet know what powers you both possess."

"Yes, I know," said Tuck. "We still don't even know who has the key?"

"I am sure that the brontosaur 'Bonds' would not have passed it on to just anyone," piped in Noelle, eyes still closed.

"I see," said Prodie in mock anger. "Listening in on other's conversations, 'ay?"

Noelle smiled and cuddled in closer to Prodie's chest.

"Try and get some rest down there," Sonki called down. "We will head out in a couple of hours when it gets a bit cooler."

Chapter 20

"Tuck...Tuck," Prodie said, giving him a lick on the cheek.

"Wha—what's up?" Tuck answered, sleepily pushing himself up onto one elbow.

"It is time to go," Sonki said, standing next to Prodie.

Ceril yawned and stretched his wings.

Tuck brushed off the grass that stuck to the side of his face, and gently shook Sienne, who was using his legs as a pillow.

Sienne opened her eyes a sliver, claws and paws filling her view. Her eyes fell shut again, but sprang open again once her brain had wrapped itself around the information it had been sent.

"No, it's not a dream," Tuck smiled, seeing the shocked look in her eyes.

Noelle stirred as Sienne scratched her behind the ear.

"Time to go?" Sienne asked, getting up.

"Yes," Sonki replied. "We have about four hours of daylight. We need to reach a safe place before nightfall."

"How can it be humid one minute and dry the next?" Sienne asked, moistening her parched lips with her tongue.

"Wind change," Sonki replied. "It is now coming in from the desert. At least the insects are forced deeper into the forest. Better drink and freshen up here. The next clean water is a while off."

"Is there something we can eat?" Tuck asked.

Prodie's ears pricked up to the mention of eating, but slumped quickly when Sonki announced that they would be able to pick berries and fruit along the way.

"There are also walnut trees in season," she added.

"Ohhh, yum, my favorite," Prodie said in a sarcastic tone as they headed to the stream to drink. Sienne splashed water onto Prodie and Noelle, while Sonki and Ceril dunked their heads in the water and ruffled their feathers.

"This water really does taste good," Tuck commented, using his shirtsleeve to wipe his face.

"No pollution, that is why," Ceril said.

"Hmm," Tuck replied absentmindedly, as he watched Prodie shake himself.

"Hey, watch it!" Ceril said as he hopped aside to miss the spray.

Prodie shot Ceril an "I'm-pleased-with-myself" grin and trotted over to Noelle.

"We can follow this stream for awhile," Sonki said as Prodie began rubbing his body on the grass. "At some point, we have to cross and head towards those hills to the west – " Sonki hesitated as she looked at the ground.

"Sonki, is there something wrong?" Sienne asked, concerned.

"No," she said, clearing her throat. "We just have to cross through Les'eat Valley."

"What's wrong with Les'eat Valley?" Tuck asked, seeing the tension in Sonki's eyes.

"That is one of the tyrannosaurs' old stomping grounds. Not a pretty site."

"You've been here before?" Sienne asked as she felt Noelle's body pushing closer to her leg.

"I have been here once or twice," replied Sonki. "I would sometimes come over with Bonds after a gathering. There is less danger when you can fly."

"*Less* danger?" Asked Tuck.

Sonki took a deep breath, looking up. "We have to move at a quick pace and stay close to the woods once we veer from the stream. I have seen pterodactyl sentries flying overhead searching for us."

Tuck and Sienne looked up to search the bright sky.

"The tyrannosaurs know that we are here, and will want to get hold of you two," Sonki said as they both stared at her.

"The pterodactyls are aligned with the T-rexes?" Tuck whispered.

"Yes," Sonki answered. "Sentra had a feeling that they would join the tyrannosaur rebels. They are not too bright and are easily led with the promise of food."

*   *   *

They walked along the stream picking berries and nuts. Sonki and Ceril flying just above the treetops ahead of them. Tuck and Sienne threw berries in the air, and they would swoop down to catch them.

"We will have to cross here," Sonki called as she landed in front of them. "The stream widens and gets deeper further on, it will be safer here. Best get another drink before we head towards Les'eat Valley."

*   *   *

From his hiding place, Yiddah watched as the group crossed the stream. He had stumbled in on their camp, almost being noticed by the hound. Not wanting to get too close to the group, he was unable to listen in on their conversations. He had never seen humans before.

"I thought humans were much taller," he thought to himself. "I wonder what they are doing here with the other sanctuary dwellers? Well, at least they are going in the same direction as me," he shrugged. He crossed the stream and followed at a safe distance careful not to be spotted by the magpies.

Chapter 21

The low sun threw long shadows as the group walked slowly across the arid plain, trying to keep close to any crop of trees or bushes they could find. The magpies kept a watchful eye in the sky for any pterodactyl.

"I think that we are being followed," Ceril whispered as he glided alongside Sonki. The heat rising up from the ground made it easy for them to keep height without any effort.

"You saw it too, then," Sonki answered.

"Shall we tell the others?" Ceril asked.

Sonki looked down. The group was trudging along in a half-sleep from the heat. "No, let them be," she said. "I will double-back in a minute and see if I can spot who is following us. Whatever it is, it is very small. Best not to take chances, though."

Yiddah watched the two magpies from behind a bush. He couldn't always see the others walking on the ground, as they often passed by low trees and bushes.

"Well, I'll just keep track of them by watching the birds," he thought to himself.

"Oh-oh, now where does he think *he* is going?" He watched as one of the magpies swooped low behind some trees and came around the other side back towards where he crouched. "Hmm, seems they suspect that someone is following them?" He questioned.

"Oh, no!" It hit him like a brontosaurus tail. "That would be *me!*"

He looked about franticly for a place to hide. He saw a small opening under a large rock. He dove under, scrambling with his hind legs to get his butt and hairy tail out of site.

With one last grunt, he pushed himself into the hole. He managed to turn himself around in the small hollow. Panting heavily, he looked through the opening, swearing under his breath at seeing the dust cloud sinking slowly around the opening.

Sonki glided over the scraggly bushes near the compi's hiding spot. She watched the settling dust cloud near a rock. She circled the rock a couple more times.

"Hmmm, could be a rats' nest," she thought to herself. "Anyway, too small to be a danger to us," she said out loud as she passed low over the rock one last time and flew off to rejoin the group.

Yiddah waited for some time then slowly squeezed himself out through the tight opening. He stood up and looked around making sure he was alone. He glanced down at the opening. "Good thing I have not eaten anything for two days," he said, patting his empty stomach.

*   *   *

Sonki landed in front of the weary travelers. "They are just children," she thought, looking at Tuck and Sienne. "What was Sentra thinking?"

"Hey, Sonki," Tuck said in a tired voice. "Do we have much further? We're really worn out down here."

"Over that rise ahead," she said, pointed with a wing, "is Les'eat Valley. There is a water hole there and some shade."

"LES'EAT?" Prodie shouted.

Everyone jumped and looked at the beagle.

"I just realized what that means!"

They all stared at him.

"What *are* you talking about?" Noelle said, annoyed.

"Do you not get it? Les'eat . . . Let's eat . . . *Let's eat!*" He said, wild eyes darting all round.

"The tyrannosaurs feeding ground!" Blurted out Sienne.

All eyes turned to Sonki.

"It should be safe there," Sonki reassured them, wings raised in a calming manner. "It *used* to be their celebration site a long time ago. It is now just a graveyard of old bones from feasts gone by."

"And they named it 'Les'eat?'" Tuck queried.

"'Let us eat' is what they used to say before starting a feast. So, after some time, they just named the valley 'Les'eat,'" Sonki explained. "Do not expect me to explain the way a tyrannosaur thinks," she quickly added, seeing the questions starting to form on their lips.

"That breed just thinks with their stomach. And, that is why

Gary B. Maier

they want to get to Earth. They will eventually make a Les'eat Valley out of the whole planet."

High above, a lone pterodactyl dipped out of a fluffy cloud and glided into another cloud.

Chapter 22

Tuck let out a low whistle as he looked up at the faded white bone ribcage once belonging to some ancient beast. The ribs curved up in an arc, almost touching as came together at the top.

"This must be at least six feet high," he shouted, standing in the midst of the ribcage with out-stretched arms.

"Can we find some water?" Prodie panted, tongue dangling out the side of his mouth.

"Yes, water," Sienne croaked through parched lips. "And shade, too."

Tuck's hands dropped limply to his side as he watched them trudge by without even as much as a sideways glance in his direction, stepping over the dried bones that littered the area

"Water and shade sounds good," he said, catching up while shooting one more glance at the remains.

"Over here," Ceril shouted from atop a large rock.

Sonki landed next to Ceril, water dripping from her tail feathers.

"It is clean," she said.

They moved quickly around the rock, Prodie and Noelle running ahead.

A small oasis opened up before them. Dense, tall bushes littered the edge of the oval pool. A cloud of yellow and red birds flew off as they stumbled to the water's edge.

Prodie jumped right in, lapping up huge gulps.

Tuck and Sienne splashed water onto their faces with Noelle lapping at the edge between them.

"Ahhh, this feels good," Sienne cooed as she took a deep drink.

"You know," Tuck began, "lately, it seems like we are always on the verge of dehydration."

"Just part of the adventure," exclaimed Prodie, shaking the water off himself.

"Why did it get so quiet all of a sudden?" Queried Sienne, water dripping from her chin.

Sonki swore under her breath and took to the air.

Ceril anxiously looked about and propelled himself off the rock to join Sonki.

"What's going on?" Sienne hissed.

Tuck bent down slowly and picked up Noelle. Her heart beat fast against his arm.

"Shhh," he froze, his ears straining to take in any little sound.

Prodie stood like a statue, ears pricked. The water dripping off his glistening coat hissed as it evaporated on the hot ground.

"Run!" Screeched Sonki from above.

From the tall bushes near the water, four tyrannosaurs stormed out towards them with huge strides.

Fan out!" Roared Mauler. "Do not let any of them get away!"

Prodie's barking shook Tuck and Sienne out of their trance.

"Move, now!" He shouted, his eyes wide with fear.

They glanced at one another, turned and ran, the tyrannosaurs' bellows ringing in their ears.

The twin tyrannosaurs Thrill and Seeker were fast and had already come up around them and now stood in the way of the fleeing group.

From behind, Mauler and Kontch bore down on them.

Sonki and Ceril began buzzing around the twins' heads, trying their best to irritate them. Seeker's head spun around like lightning. He clamped his jaws down onto Ceril's wing. Ceril let out a painful screech as Seeker shook his head from side to side.

"Ceril!" Sonki shrieked in horror. She dove down at Seeker, her beak spearing Seeker's hide just below his left eye. Seeker howled, his eye tearing up as Ceril fluttered limply to the ground.

"Tuck!" Sienne yelled as she stumbled over some loose bones.

"Come on," he said, helping her up. "We can make it to those trees."

"You are not going anywhere," Mauler growled from above them.

Panting, they gazed helplessly at the huge rows of jagged, meat-encrusted incisors.

Prodie growled, bearing his own teeth.

"Cool it, mutt, or I will eat you right now," growled Mauler, glaring down his long leathery face at the dog. "Grab the two humans," he ordered.

"No!" Shouted Tuck, as the twin tyrannosaurs moved towards them. Tuck and Sienne both threw their hands up instinctively. A shimmering dome suddenly appeared, seemingly out of nowhere, shielding the group from the tyrannosaurs. They could barely hear the muted growls of the confused tyrannosaurs as the beasts repeatedly head-butted the shield.

"Where did *this* come from?" Exclaimed Sienne, watching in bewilderment as the tyrannosaurs moved on to attempting to bite their way through the shield.

"I don't know," answered Tuck without turning away from the bizarre spectacle playing out above him. "But, I get the distinct feeling we probably shouldn't put our hands down."

"Look," Noelle said, pointing with one small paw. They turned just in time to see Sonki dragging Ceril with her beak into a bush. Sonki paused to give a reassuring nod in their direction, and then disappeared.

"So, what do we do now?" Questioned Sienne.

"I don't know," Tuck winced, his arms quaking with every assault on the shield by the tyrannosaurs. "All I know, is we can't hold this up for much longer."

The tyrannosaurs suddenly stopped their assault and started walking slowly around the shield. The muffled sound of their anguished voices barely seeped through.

"My arms are getting heavy," Sienne croaked in pain. Sweat was running down Tuck's face. His arms were shaking.

"We could make a break for it," Prodie said. "Those trees are not that far away. All we would need was a little distraction."

"How are we going to distract them from *in here?*" Noelle asked nervously.

The tyrannosaurs continued their lumbering procession around the shield. Mauler looked directly at Tuck with one yellow eye, an evil grin forming on his face as he watched the beads of sweat run down Tuck's cheeks.

Without warning, the hulking beasts all turned their heads upwards, as if being called. Mauler barked orders and the twins turned away and stomped towards the water.

"Now!" Yelled Prodie. "We have to make a run for it *now.*"

"Okay," said Tuck. "We'll split up . . ."

"No, we can't," Sienne panted, her arms quaking with adrenalin.

"We don't have a choice," Tuck shouted. "We have a better chance now that there are only two of them. Take Noelle, and I will go with Prodie. Get to the trees, we'll meet around the other side of the oasis."

"But . . ." Sienne looked at the backs of distracted tyrannosaurs, distorted by the shield.

"Just go – while these two T-rexes are still watching the smaller ones. On three, drop your hands, run – and don't look back!"

Sienne stared at Tuck, eyes wide with panic.

"It will be alright," he said, surprised by how calm his voice sounded to himself. "Ready?"

She nodded. Noelle crawled up her leg and clung onto her shirt.

"One . . . two . . . *three!*"

They both dropped their arms. The shield evaporated as they sprinted in opposite directions.

"There are making a run for it," roared Kontch as he tore off after Sienne. Mauler swore in a language alien at Sienne as he turned and ran after Kontch. Kontch easily caught up with Sienne, lowered his head and nudged Sienne roughly in the back. Sienne fell forwards, sprawling face-first into the dirt. She cried out in pain as the weight of Kontch's log-sized middle toe pressed down upon her leg.

"Do not try to get up," he snarled. "Or, I will push harder."

"Where is the other human?" Mauler asked as he gazed down at his prize.

"I did not see him," Kontch answered.

Mauler's scaly upper lip arched as he hissed, "They must have split up."

"Shall I fetch the twins and search for him?"

"No. We'll take this one to Thorn. This will at least make him pleased with us for a change."

"Get up," Mauler commanded, as Kontch lifted the clawed toe from Sienne's leg.

Sienne stood up slowly, stuffing Noelle under her shirt. She looked up at the tyrannosaur.

"Try and run and I will squash you like a toadstool," Mauler warned her in a low rumble. His breath smelled like mildew and beef jerky. "Do you understand?"

Sienne nodded faster than she had intended.

"Now, move."

Sienne started walking, favoring her left leg. She hugged Noelle tight to her rib cage.

On the far side of the oasis, Tuck and Prodie watched as the tyrannosaurs trudged away with Sienne as their prisoner. They could just make out the terrifying silhouettes of Thrill and Seeker as they made their way back to join Mauler and Kontch. Tears made rivulets down Tuck's dusty face. A low whine escaped from Prodie's quivering maw.

Chapter 23

"What do we do now?" Prodie asked in a whimper.

Tuck didn't answer. Tears were still streaming down his face. "What the heck have we gotten ourselves into?" He finally said. "Those were real dinosaurs, and now they have Sienne and Noelle."

"I know where they are taking them," came a voice from behind them.

"What the – " Tuck shouted, spinning around just in time for Prodie, who had leapt into the air in fright, to clamp firmly onto his head.

"Prodie, get off!" Tuck yelled from where he had toppled backwards onto the ground, trying frantically to pry the panicked dog from his head. Prodie's paws remained tightly wrapped around Tuck's neck.

Yiddah stood quietly for a few moments, watching with amusement as the human struggled in vain with the beagle-shaped helmet.

"I will just wait until you two are finished with your mating ritual, shall I?" He said.

Tuck and Prodie froze, mid-struggle. Tuck squinted out from under one of Prodie's floppy brown ears. From his perspective, Tuck had to tilt his sneakers to make a V, revealing a small hairy-looking dinosaur, about one foot in height, with a long skinny neck and an Emu-like head cocked to one side, staring intently at them.

"You are a compsognathus, are you not?" Prodie asked, gazing at Yiddah. He still sat on Tuck's chest, his tail swatting Tuck's nose as it wagged in greeting.

"He's a what?" Tuck said, pushing Prodie to the ground next to him and sitting up.

He tried unsuccessfully to brush the mixture of Prodie fur and prehistoric twigs and leaves from his shirt and hair.

"You're a what?" He asked again, this time, addressing Yiddah directly.

"I am called Yiddah," the small brown creature said. "I am a compsognathus from the woods clan. We are usually called 'compis' because the full name can be a tongue twister. So," he said, looking at Tuck with one large, yellow eye, "You must be one of the human key masters."

"And you know that how?" Tuck said, a shocked look on his face.

"Because the tyrannosaurs are after me, too. They want this." He opened one small-clawed hand to reveal a shimmering blue-green disc.

Prodie trotted forward to get a closer look at the disc. "It is the key to Earth!" He exclaimed, turning to Tuck. Prodie looked back at Yiddah. "But – but, how did you get this?" He asked.

"A brontosaur. I think his name was Bonds. He gave it to me and then disappeared. He did not look well. Since then, the tyrannosaurs have been hunting me. They attacked my village and are holding my mother prisoner in their lair. That is probably where they will take the human girl too. So, what are you two called?"

"Sorry. I'm Tuck, and this is Prodie," Tuck answered, getting to his knees and shaking Yiddah's leathery hand. "Were you the one who distracted the T-rexes back there?"

"Yes, I have been following you for a while. I had to be certain about your intentions before I revealed myself. The magpie almost saw me."

"Oh, no!" Tuck cried, remembering. "Ceril!" He took off in a sprint out of the brush.

"What is wrong?" Yiddah asked Prodie as they ran after Tuck.

"Ceril, one of the magpies. He was injured by a tyrannosaur."

"Sonki," Tuck called as he crouched down near the bush where he had seen them disappear.

Sonki emerged from the bush just as Prodie and Yiddah joined them. Sonki eyed Yiddah suspiciously.

"That's Yiddah," Tuck said. "He helped us escape from the T-rexes. But, they have Sienne and Noelle," he added, looking at the ground in despair.

"I know," Sonki answered. "I saw everything."

"How is Ceril?" Tuck asked, his brow furled.

"He is still unconscious. His wing is badly damaged. I will have to stay here with him until he is strong enough to travel."

71

"I will get a message to my clan and have someone come and tend to your friend and take you somewhere safe," said Yiddah.

"Thank you," said Sonki, gratitude showing in her eyes. She looked at Tuck. "I am sorry that I will not be able to help you further."

"That's okay. It's more important that you keep Ceril safe. Yiddah here will help us get to the T-rexes' lair."

Sonki gave Yiddah a curious look.

"Bonds gave *you* the key to Earth, did he not?" She asked.

"Yes. The tyrannosaurs also know that I have the key. They are holding my mother captive. That is how I stumbled upon you lot."

"So, that was you following us, then?" Sonki asked.

"Yeah. For a moment, I thought you had spotted me at that hole under the rock."

"I saw the settling dust. I do not see how you managed to get through that opening," Sonki said, looking Yiddah up and down."

"Hey, I have not eaten in two days," he grinned, showing a tiny row of razor-sharp teeth and patting his growling tummy.

"Ah-hem," Tuck said, clearing his throat. We should settle here for the night. I don't think that the T-rexes will be coming back any time soon."

"Sounds good," replied Prodie. "We all need some rest, and we can head out early in the morning before the heat settles in."

"Let's not stay too close to the water," said Yiddah. "This is the only water hole for a day's travel, never know who might show up in the dark."

"Sounds good," answered Prodie.

"There are some nice low overhanging trees just on the other side of this bush," Sonki said. "Should keep anyone from spotting us."

"Alright, then. Let's make ourselves comfortable." Tuck bent down to check on Ceril's wing. "I think it's broken," he said as he ran a finger lightly along the wing. "I'll go to the pond and get some water and maybe find something to make a splint for his wing."

"I will go with you," Yiddah offered. "Just to watch out for anything big that might like to eat you," he grinned again.

"Great," muttered Tuck. "That's just what we need. Another bloody comedian."

"Heckova sight," said Prodie. I wish I had one of those human picture-taking devices. Not something you see everyday, dinosaurs and humans working together."

They both laughed.

Chapter 24

"There," Tuck said, gently tying a knot out of dried reed across the splint on Ceril's wing. "That should do it."

Ceril groaned, his small body shifting with discomfort.

"Ceril," Sonki cried, jumping to his side. "How do you feel?"

Ceril opened his eyes a sliver, looking up at the concerned faces.

"Who is the skinny dude?" He croaked, closing his eyes again.

"I am called 'Yiddah,'" Yiddah answered. "So, what is your next trick going to be, arm-wrestling a brontosaur?"

Ceril laughed, wincing in pain.

"Feeling better, then," Tuck said. "You gave us quite a scare back there."

"Where is Sienne?" Ceril asked, looking about.

They all looked at one another, each not wanting to be the one to give the bad news.

"Is she – " Ceril began, trying to get up.

"No, she's not," Tuck said, gently placing a finger against Ceril's downy chest. The T-rexes have her . . . and Noelle."

"We must save them!" Ceril cried.

"*You* are not going anywhere," Sonki said sternly.

"But – " the injured bird sputtered.

"No buts," Tuck said. "Sonki will stay here with you until you are well enough to travel. Yiddah here is going to send word to his clan. They'll come and help you both to safety."

Ceril opened his beak to protest.

"You did good back there," Prodie said, giving Ceril a lick on the head. "But, in this condition, you will only slow us down and hurt yourself more."

Ceril leaned back, deflated. He realized the truth in Prodie's words.

"Yiddah here will show us the way to the tyrannosaurs' lair," Prodie continued.

"Let's get some rest," Tuck said. "We'll need to have our wits about us tomorrow."

"Too right," sighed Prodie as he began to make a nest in the grass next to Ceril.

Tuck lay down on his back. He gazed up through the trees at the stars.

Yiddah squatted down like a chicken and studied Tuck, seeing easily with his night vision.

"Sure are a lot of bright stars out tonight," Tuck said, hands folded behind his head.

Yiddah looked up at the night sky. "I hear stories that there are as many humans on Earth now as there are stars in the sky."

Tuck turned his head to meet the two shining eyes breaking Yiddah's dark silhouette.

"I also hear that there are still some of our ancestor's living on Earth who survived the Long Winter."

"Yes, there are seven billion people now living on Earth," Tuck answered.

"Hmm, no wonder the tyrannosaurs want to get down there. Lots to eat."

"Yes," agreed Sonki. "And with the ability to jump in and out of sanctuaries, it would be difficult for the humans to stop them, even with their powerful weapons."

"Not a pretty picture," Yiddah said, emitting a low whistle.

"Sentra suspects that the dinosaurs on Earth maybe working with the tyrannosaurs here," Sonki added.

"Well, either way," said Tuck, "I doubt the sanctuary dwellers would want any powerful corrupt humans to get the key to the sanctuaries. They would turn all these places into zoos or game hunting for profit."

"Sounds like the tyrannosaurs *should* be able to do a little feeding down there, then," Yiddah replied.

"I wouldn't have anything against it," Tuck chuckled.

"Be careful what you wish for," said Prodie.

"Only joking," Tuck said. "Besides, the bad humans probably wouldn't taste any good."

Their laughter hung in the night air.

Chapter 25

Sienne pushed herself up the rough steep stairs, the pain in her left leg throbbing in time with her labored breathing.

"Keep moving," Mauler growled, roughly nudging her forward.

"My leg hurts!" She yelled up to him.

"My leg hurts," he mocked. "I hope the meat on you is as soft as your backbone," he added, grinning.

The laugh from Kontch and the twins echoed up the stairs. Sienne cursed herself for showing weakness.

"More than your leg will be hurting when we are done with you,

I can promise you that," she said, staring defiantly up at Mauler.

"I wonder why the smallest creatures always have to puff themselves up to something they are not," came a deep growl from the shadows.

Sienne spun around, taking an involuntary step back. A cold shiver ran down her spine.

Thorn's huge head emerged from the dark. He bent down low to Sienne, looking at her with one large, bloodshot eye.

"So, this is an all-powerful key master," he grumbled, looking her up and down. "You do not look like much," he added, visibly disappointed.

"Where is the other one?" He asked, turning his attention to Mauler.

"Well, he got away," Mauler answered, head bowed. "They have help from other sanctuary dwellers," he added quickly.

Thorn thought a moment, considering a punishment for their failure. "Hmmm," he finally said.

Kontch and the twins gave one another looks of puzzlement and relief.

"Throw her in with the lizard," Thorn ordered. "We need to prepare." He turned and disappeared into the darkened hallway.

Mauler shoved Sienne along the hallway. "You heard. Move."

"In here," he said, motioning with his head at an entrance to the left.

She walked through the dark entrance, and then the floor disappeared. She screamed as she fell onto a bed of dried grass.

The laughter of the retreating tyrannosaurs echoed throughout the hallway.

Sienne sat up, spitting hay from her mouth. She waited for her eyes to adjust to the dark. A small opening high above gave a small sliver of light. Not enough for her to see very well.

"Something else is in here with us," whispered Noelle, climbing out of Sienne's shirt.

"What?" Sienne hissed, squinting in the darkness.

A slight rustling came from the far corner.

"What is it?" Sienne asked under her breath, straining her eyes to see.

Two small glowing eyes shone at them from the dark.

"It looks to be injured," answered Noelle, her eyes seeing better in the dark. "I will go and see if it needs help."

"Wait!" Exclaimed Sienne.

Sienne crawled after Noelle to where the small creature lay.

Noelle looked over the frail body. Her eyes paused on the broken leg that was showing serious infection.

"Who are you?" Noelle asked.

The creature's eyes opened a sliver. "My name is Yenzl," she croaked. "I am from the woods clan of the compis. The tyrannosaurs attacked us and I was taken here. I think I heard them say that they were after my son, Yiddah. I do not know what they want with him, he is such a good boy." Her eyes fell shut again.

"My name is Noelle and this is Sienne from Earth."

"A *human?*" Yenzl rasped. "What is a human doing here?"

"It's a long story," Sienne said, her eyes finally having adjusted somewhat.

"How long have you been in here?"

"I think since yesterday, but I am not sure."

"Is there any water in here?" Sienne asked, looking about.

"There is a small troth near the entrance," Yenzl pointed with a quivering claw.

Sienne went over and came back with part of her shirtsleeve soaked with water. She knelt down and gently proceeded to clean the wound.

"That feels good," sighed Yenzl.

"Noelle, see if you can find some strong twigs. We should try and splint this leg."

"Okay," Noelle said as she scurried off.

Yenzl watched as Sienne tore off a piece of her shirt and wrapped it around her leg.

"I hear bad stories about you humans," Yenzl commented.

Sienne looked at Yenzl. "Yes, there are some not-so-nice humans," she replied.

"You seem to be nice, though."

"Thanks."

"Here, will this do," Noelle said as she dropped twigs from her mouth.

Sienne rifled through the twigs, picking five sturdy ones. "Well done," she said to Noelle. "We can place these around the break and tie them gently. That should give the break support and maybe allow it to mend itself properly. Sorry, I am not too good at this," she said as she tied the twigs in place.

"It feels much better now, thank you," Yenzl said, placing her small leathery hand on Sienne's arm.

Chapter 26

"We now have one of the key masters," Thorn announced with pride, returning to Ka'Dilla's side.

"That is good news, my dear," Ka'Dilla said, nuzzling her nose to his neck.

Tusker watched his mother crooning over Thorn. He did not think it wise for her to give herself up so quickly to him. Thorn had gotten bored quickly with other mates in the past, and they usually didn't live to tell about it.

"Something troubling you?" Zahar asked, observing Tusker watching Thorn and Ka'dilla nuzzling, his eyes glowing from under his hood.

Tusker ignored the wolf as he watched Thorn nibble on his mother's neck.

"We had better get the ability to reach Earth soon," Zahar said with a little added sarcasm. "Or Thorn might take his impatience out on some one close."

"Shut up, wolf!" Tusker growled, focusing an eye on Zahar. Hate oozed from his stare.

"I think that it is time for you to open the gate to your sanctuary," Tusker said with an evil grin. "And let us deal with your council members so that you and your clan can start scouting on Earth."

Zahar cocked his head slightly, eyeing the tyrannosaur. "This one might be even more dangerous than Thorn," he thought to himself.

The laughter echoing from Mauler, Kontch and the twins coming from the hall entrance broke the intensity between them.

"You should have heard the human scream as it fell into the pit," Kontch exclaimed excitedly.

Mauler and the twins took a couple of steps back as Thorn rounded on Kontch.

"You will be the first through the gate to Earth," he spat.

The happiness on Kontch's face disappeared faster than a fish down a pterodactyl's gullet.

"What is the use of just one key master?" Zahar asked dryly. "We need both to open the gate to Earth," he added.

Thorn stared with annoyance at the wolf.

"Well, wolf," Thorn began, his voice even. "Since it looks like the compis are not attempting to retrieve their missing female, I am sure that the other key master will be coming to save its mate. I am told . . . " he glanced at Mauler, " . . . that the key masters have help from other sanctuary dwellers."

"That will probably be Sentra's doing," Zahar interjected. "Sentra is also likely to be in possession of the key that the brontosaur Bonds passed on to that compi. So we must capture the other human."

"How many are in the group, and where are they now?" Zahar asked Mauler.

Mauler glanced at Thorn, unsure whether he should answer.

"Answer him," growled Thorn.

"They are at Les'eat Valley. There is maybe four or five altogether. Seeker here killed one of the birds in the group."

Thorn grunted.

"There is something else," Mauler began hesitantly.

"What is it?" Asked Zahar.

"As we attacked and had them surrounded, the key masters somehow put up an invisible shield that we were not able to penetrate. That is why we were not able to get them all."

"What do you mean, they put up an invisible shield?" Bellowed Thorn, baring his teeth in rage.

"Wait!" Exclaimed Zahar. "I have heard of this." He scratched his chin with his paw and thought a moment.

Thorn growled his impatience as he glared at Zahar.

"We were told stories from long ago," Zahar finally said. "The last time the key master's aid was needed. They also had powers we sanctuary dwellers did not know of, and if I remember the stories correctly, neither did the key masters.

"Now, wait a minute!" Exclaimed Thorn. "I have heard these same stories. That the key masters had . . . have," he corrected himself, "Powers is common in our folklore. But you are saying that they do not know *what* powers they posses?"

"Exactly!" Zahar answered. "It must have been just a coincidence that they conjured up an invisible dome at that precise moment. Also, if my memory is true, the key masters have to be united to be able to use any powers they posses."

"Hmmm," mused Thorn. "That is good news," he grinned.

"They are camped less than a day away," Thorn said. "At first light, have the pterodactyl fly over that area and keep watch of their movements," he barked at the twins.

"Of course," they replied, bowing.

"We will have a nice welcome prepared for their arrival," he said, rubbing his tiny hands together in anticipation.

Chapter 27

Tuck awoke to whimpering sounds. Prodie was having a dream, his hind legs kicking as he whimpered.

He looked over at Sonki, who was still sleeping, her beak tucked deep under her wing. Ceril, lying next to Sonki, seemed to be breathing normally. Tuck looked about for Sienne, his heart picking up pace. Then, yesterday's events came thundering from the back of his brain. "We have to get them back!" He thought to himself, adrenaline pumping through his body. Voices coming through from the other side of the bushes halted Tuck's breathing. He strained to hear, looking about. "Where's Yiddah?" He thought.

Tuck quietly stood up and parted some of the foliage to see Yiddah talking to something that looked like a vulture that had been through the wringer. Grey scraggly feathers pointing in all directions, a thorny head with red bug eyes atop a short bald neck and long spindly legs with claws that played with the dirt. The creature stopped talking as it looked in Tuck's direction. "Looks like your human friend is awake," it said.

Yiddah turned towards Tuck. "Come over and meet my friend," he said.

Tuck squeezed through the bushes and walked over to them.

"This is Eejh, from one of the Vulture clans in this area," Yiddah said.

"Vulture, aye?" Tuck said, extending his hand. "I'm Tuck. Your kind hasn't changed much in these past few million years," he smiled.

Eejh shook Tuck's hand with his wing. "Funny-looking thing, are you not?" He said, giving Tuck the once over.

"He is okay," Yiddah chuckled. "Eejh, here will be flying back to my clan to bring someone back to help Ceril."

"That's very kind of you," Tuck said graciously.

"No problem. I was just telling Yiddah here that you must watch out for pterodactyls. I have seen them patrolling the skies over Les'eat Valley since sunup."

Tuck looked up to the blue sky that was dotted with fluffy white clouds.

"The tyrannosaurs know that we are coming," Yiddah began. "And will be waiting for us."

"And we will be ready for them," Prodie huffed as he emerged from the bushes.

"Looks like there are all sorts of strange creatures here today," Eejh said, eyeing Prodie.

"We have beaten them once before, and we will beat them again," Prodie said with gusto.

"Yes, how *did* you manage to put up that invisible barrier against the tyrannosaurs?" Yiddah asked with curiosity.

"I really don't know," Tuck answered, shrugging his shoulders. "I – that is – Sienne and I instinctively put up our hands when the T-rexes attacked and it just appeared. Sentra told us that we have powers. I guess that is one of them."

"So, what *else* can you do?" Yiddah pressed.

"We don't know. I just know that we have to be together for the powers to work."

"That is not much help," Yiddah exclaimed.

"Anyway," Eejh interrupted. "I will leave you all to figure this out, and go get help for your bird friend."

"Okay. Thanks, Eejh," Yiddah said.

"Yes, thanks again," said Tuck.

"No worries," replied Eejh. "Someone will be here before the darkness." He bent his legs and kicked off, his two-meter wingspan kicking up dust as he gained height.

They all followed Eejh's progress until he entered a cloud and disappeared.

"The wind has changed. There will be a storm coming soon," announced Yiddah, sniffing towards the east.

Above the horizon, thick dark clouds were closing in on the sun.

"That will be good for us," Tuck said. "Harder for the pterodactyl to spot us."

"I do not know what the storms are like on Earth, but here you had better be under strong shelter before it hits. Very electrical . . . and not much rain."

"Then, we had better get going," Tuck said. "Let's get Sonki and Ceril to a safer place, and then we can head out."

"Sounds good," said Prodie.

Tuck gently carried Ceril to a nearby hollowed out stump with Sonki hopping along behind.

"The two of you will be safe here," he said, putting Ceril gently on a patch of dried grass. "Help is already on the way. They should be here by nightfall."

"The storm should pass by quickly," Yiddah added, noticing Sonki looking at the darkening horizon.

Ceril groaned. "Just get Sienne and Noelle back," he said weakly.

"We will," Prodie said, giving Ceril a lick on the head.

"Be careful," Sonki said, concern breaking her voice. "The tyrannosaurs are very dangerous."

"All will be good," Tuck assured her. "We have Yiddah here to show us the way. Plus, we have to get his mother out too," he said with a smile.

A rumbling in the distance got their attention and they moved out into the clearing. Yiddah looked into the sky to see if all was clear.

"Hard to tell if we are being watched with the increase in cloud cover," he said.

"There are some caves in a hillside about two hour's walk from here. We should make it before the storm hits."

"Okay. Let's move out, then," said Tuck. "We'll just have to take our chances. Maybe the oncoming storm will ground the pterodactyl, as well," he added hopefully.

"Alright," Yiddah began. "Follow me. I will try to keep as much as possible to tree cover. But it will not get any thicker where we are going."

The trio headed out. Prodie gave Sonki and Ceril one more look, turned and joined Tuck and Yiddah.

"May you all be safe," Sonki whispered, as she watched them disappear behind the thick bushes.

Chapter 28

A pterodactyl glided between the gathering clouds as it watched the strange creatures below briskly walking towards the tyrannosaur lair. The wind picked up and the pterodactyl adjusted its wings to compensate for the buffeting gusts. Thunder was loud and coming close as lightning bolts leapt from cloud to cloud.

"Hmmm. Maybe I should report their position to Thorn before I lose them in the storm," it thought to itself as it warily eyed a lightning bolt streaking across its path.

*   *   *

Yiddah watched the pterodactyl as it dipped in and out of the clouds.

"We should pick up the pace," he said. "The storm is moving in faster than I expected."

"Okay," Tuck answered as he and Prodie hustled to keep up with Yiddah.

"How much further?" Tuck asked, jogging beside Yiddah.

"Those hills up ahead," Yiddah pointed.

"Dang!" Tuck exclaimed. He looked up to the sky to see the thick dark clouds enveloping the sun. "Let's move it."

Frightened by a loud crackle of thunder, Prodie bolted out ahead, tail between his legs, chuckles from Tuck and Yiddah followed.

Exploding rock from a lightning strike behind them erased the smiles off their faces and they quickly caught up with Prodie.

The wind howled as it pushed them towards the caves, dust and debris of dried twigs and grass pummeling their bodies.

"Hurry!" Yiddah cried, as they scrambled up the slope.

Lightning bolts crashed into trees and rocks around them as dove into the opening of a cave.

*   *   *

The pterodactyl dove out of the clouds, while gusts of wind toyed with its wings as it desperately attempted to maintain its balance against the storm. It sped down to Earth, a flurry of lightning crisscrossing in its path. The pterodactyl dodged through the searing white bolts as the ground came up to meet it. With a loud clap of thunder, a white bolt shot from the clouds, punching a hole through the pterodactyl's right wing.

The scream from the pterodactyl was lost in the storm as it spiraled to the ground. Dust clouds rose where it fell and were whisked away with the wind, leaving the groaning pterodactyl alone with the elements.

* * *

The thunder echoed through the cave as lightning flashes lit up the cave's interior. Tuck, Yiddah and Prodie huddled together in the back of the cave, staring wide-eyed at the opening as lightning wreaked havoc with anything in its path.

Then, suddenly, silence. Tuck held his breath, his ears pricked, nothing. Dead silence.

"What happened?" He asked.

Yiddah stood up and dusted himself off. "Storm has past," he said, as he walked out of the cave, sunlight lighting up the entrance. Tuck and Prodie slowly stuck their heads out. The wind was gone, no sign of clouds. Birds were chirping as if the storm never happened.

"Weird," announced Prodie, sniffing the air.

"You're not wrong," agreed Tuck.

"Well, I do not see any pterodactyl," Yiddah said surveying the sky. "Either they went back to the tyrannosaurs lair, or the storm got them."

They walked down the slope. Tuck whistled in awe at all the splintered trees that littered the area, some smoldering from where the lightning had struck.

"This will make the going a little harder," he commented.

"Then, we have no time to lose," Yiddah said, zigzagging through the debris.

Prodie easily navigated the maze as Tuck swore, stumbling over rocks and branches.

* * *

The Pterodactyl dragged itself to a nearby bush as the strange creatures walked in its direction. It lay still as they walked passed its

Gary B. Maier

refuge, not daring to breathe, lest the hound notice it. The pterodactyl let out its breath as they moved on.

"I must find a safe place to hide," it murmured. "Too many hungry creatures in this area."

Chapter 29

The tyrannosaurs glanced nervously towards the high ceiling as lightning flashed around the structure. Crackling thunder echoed throughout the hall. Ka'dilla huddled by Thorn, her body shivering each time lightning struck. Thorn did not like these storms, but could not allow his nerves to show as his eyes met with Zahar's staring out from under his hood.

*   *   *

"It is a lightning storm," Yenzl said as lightning lit up their prison. "It will be over soon."

Sienne walked over to the entrance as another bolt of lightning lit up the room.

She could see the ledge she had just fallen from. Sienne jumped up, her hand just reaching the lip of the ledge.

"It's no use, it's too high for me to get out," she sighed, walking back to Yenzl and Noelle.

"Would you be able to hoist me over the top?" Noelle asked. "I could then go and warn the others before they get here."

"Hmm," considered Sienne. "That could work. The ledge is only about six feet high."

"But there are sentries at the bottom of the stairs," interjected Yenzl, concerned.

"I know," said Noelle. "I am sure that they will be hiding from the storm, though. We would have to do this now, *before* the storm passes. The tyrannosaurs do not even know that I am here. I will not be missed."

"It won't be easy," Sienne said with a worried look. "Those steps are very steep, and you might get caught."

"I will be okay," Noelle said with conviction. "We have to warn Tuck and Prodie that the tyrannosaurs know they are coming."

"Yes, you're right," Sienne agreed. "We're only being used as bait. The T-rexes need both me and Tuck to get to Earth. I'm guessing that means they haven't found the key that Bonds the brontosaurus passed on before he died. Otherwise, we wouldn't be needed and most likely be killed," she swallowed, " – or eaten."

"Okay," Noelle said, meeting everyone's eyes. "Not a pleasant thought. Shall we get going?"

Noelle climbed into Sienne's cupped hands.

"Ready?" Sienne asked.

"As ready as one can be," Noelle said, taking a deep breath.

Sienne hoisted Noelle up over the edge as lightning lit up the entrance. Noelle disappeared over the lip. A moment later, her head reappeared over the edge, her whiskers twitching.

"All good," she said.

"Okay. Be careful," Sienne hissed.

"Can you get a message to my clan that I am still alive?" Yenzl asked nervously.

"I will see what I can do," Noelle answered.

"How will you even find Tuck and Prodie?" Sienne suddenly asked.

"I shall keep to the high ground and watch out for them."

"Be careful."

"I will."

Noelle's snout disappeared as thunder clapped loudly overhead. She hugged the rough wall as more lightning lit up the hallway.

*   *   *

Zahar's keen ears picked up a scratching sound that did not belong to the storm. His eyes glowed from under the hood as he focused his gaze on the hallway.

"There!" He said to himself. A small creature was scurrying along the wall towards the stairs. "Did we miss something?" He asked himself. He bolted towards the entrance just as the small creature disappeared down the staircase.

"Where are you going, wolf?" Thorn called after him.

Zahar ignored him as he reached the stairs. He peered over the first step to see the white and grey colored rat reach the fourth step. Zahar bounded down the stairs, jumping over Noelle and halting on the step below her.

"And where do *you* think you are going?" Zahar said, flaring his teeth, as he spun to face her.

Noelle and the wolf's eyes met briefly as she dove to escape between Zahar's legs.

"I do not think so," the wolf growled as he snapped and fastened his jaws around Noelle's neck.

Noelle let out a loud squeal of pain.

"Noelle!" Sienne cried, hearing Noelle's pained shriek.

Zahar tightened his grip on Noelle's neck, closing her windpipe as she struggled.

Slowly, her body went limp and hung in Zahar's mouth like a rag doll.

"Noelle!" Sienne called again, franticly jumping up to try and see over the ledge.

Zahar's head appeared over the edge. Sienne took one step back as lightning lit up Noelle's body hanging lifeless from the jaws protruding from under a hood, the wolf's eyes glowing menacingly. Sienne stared, stunned. Without a word, Zahar turned and was gone.

"Noelle!" Sienne cried out, falling to her knees, sobbing.

*　　　*　　　*

"Sienne!" Tuck shouted.

"What?" Prodie yelped, startled at Tuck's outburst.

"It's Sienne!" Tuck said, sweat running down his face.

"Sienne is what?" Prodie asked cautiously.

"Something has happened to Noelle!"

"What do you mean, something has happened to Noelle?" Prodie asked, placing his front paws on Tuck's knees.

"I felt Sienne's pain for Noelle," he said, crouching down to Prodie's height.

"You *felt* this?" Yiddah asked.

"I can't explain it," Tuck answered. "I just now felt it. It's like our minds are somehow connected."

"Do you think it is possible for you to contact Sienne in the same way?" Yiddah asked.

Tuck looked at Yiddah, considering this.

"Yes, maybe if you concentrate, you could talk to her," Prodie exclaimed.

"You mean like mental telepathy?" Tuck said.

"Why not," Yiddah said, shrugging his shouders.

Tuck looked from Prodie to Yiddah. "Alright, I'll give it a try."

Tuck sat down and folded his legs. He closed his eyes and called out Sienne's name in his mind.

*   *   *

Sienne stopped sobbing when she heard Tuck calling for her.

"Tuck!" She said out loud.

Chapter 30

Zahar unclenched his jaws, letting Noelle drop to the floor.

"I hate rats!" Zahar said with disgust as he spat out fur. "It seems we missed something. It was trying to escape."

Thorn gazed down at the rat with disinterest. "Is it dead?" He asked.

"No, only unconscious," Zahar answered.

"Kill it," Thorn said to the twins.

Licking his yellow teeth, Seeker tilted his massive head sideways as he lowered it to pick up the little morsel.

Noelle opened her eyes just a sliver. The wolf was distracted, talking to the tyrannosaurs. She carefully looked about for an escape. There. Along the opposite wall was a small opening. "Hopefully, it will be big enough for me," she thought.

She bolted for the gap in the wall just as the tyrannosaur was about to scoop her up into his putrid jaws.

"What the...!" Exclaimed Seeker, his teeth clamping down on air.

"Get it!" Zahar shouted.

Thrill and Kontch lurched after Noelle with huge strides, their bellows echoing off the walls. Noelle scurried into the opening just before a huge leg slammed down in front of the gap. Noelle shrieked as the end of her tail was ripped off. Breathing heavily, she took her tail into her hands. "Better than all of me," she thought, licking the bloodied end. She leapt back when a sleek black paw reached in through the hole, stamping about and missing her by inches.

Noelle looked franticly around the small space for a passageway. Nothing.

"Well, I seem to be cornered like a rat," she mumbled, before cursing herself for using the human phrase. A single claw brushed her fur as she pressed herself up against the back of the tiny cavern. The paw retreated and was replaced with a single glowing eye glaring from the opening.

"You will die in here, rat," Zahar's voice hissed through the opening, smelling like secrets and hate.

"It will not be going anywhere," Zahar said, turning to Kontch. "There is no other way out."

"The storm has passed," Thorn said, looking at the sunlight creeping through the small windows high in the walls. "The pterodactyl should be reporting in soon of the progress of the other human."

"That is, if the storm did not get it," Zahar added.

Thorn glared at the wolf. "You are right," he finally said.

"Thrill, Seeker, go to the top of the tower and keep a look out for the human. And, for the pterodactyl," he added, staring at Zahar.

Thrill and Seeker gave each other nervous looks as they slowly headed for the stairs to the tower.

"I hate it up there," Seeker said under his breath to Thrill. "I get dizzy when I look down."

"I will go up there," Thrill answered, a bead of sweat running down his snout. "But I will not be looking down either, or I will throw up.

"Let us just sit there and look for the Pterodactyl," Seeker said. "I am sure that it will be back soon and we can get down from here." Their eyes slowly adjusted to the bright sunlight as they slumped against the wall of the tower.

"You were bested by a rat," Thrill sniggered.

"Shut up!" Seeker said, annoyed. He lunged for Thrill's neck. Thrill swung his tail around, knocking the wind out of Seeker as he crashed into the opposite wall.

"Now, stay put before Thorn comes up and throws us both off the tower," Thrill said, looking nervously down the stairway.

Seeker caught his breath and settled himself. "At least, I caught that magpie in midflight," he said proudly.

"Whatever," Thrill mumbled and began searching the sky for signs of the pterodactyl.

Chapter 31

"Tuck! Is that you? Where are you?" Sienne hissed, her eyes darting about in the darkness.

"Don't talk, think the words," Tuck said, his voice soothing.

"What?" She said out loud.

"Don't say the words out loud. Use your mind," he said, this time not as calm.

"Whom are you talking to?" Yenzl asked, looking at her curiously.

"Ahhh, no one," Sienne lied. "Hang on a minute," she added confused.

"Tuck," she said, this time in her mind.

"Finally," Tuck said, relieved.

"How are you doing this?" She asked.

"What has happened to Noelle?" Prodie badgered, breaking Tuck's concentration.

"I don't know yet," Tuck said opening his eyes. "Let me talk to Sienne and I will find out what's going on."

Prodie lay down, head resting on his front paws with big concerned chocolate eyes watching Tuck.

Tuck closed his eyes again. "Is everything alright?" He asked. "I heard you scream and felt that something had happened to Noelle. Is she alright?"

"No, she isn't," she replied, her voice shaking. Something got her. I think it was a wolf. I don't know if she is alive," she sobbed.

"What happened?" Tuck asked.

"She tried to make an escape to warn you that the T-rexes know you're coming."

"We know they know. There has been a pterodactyl watching us, but we haven't seen it since the storm. Are you okay?"

"I'm fine. I'm in some sort of dudgeon with another small creature."

"That must be Yiddah's mother."

"Who's Yiddah?

"We ran into him just after you were captured. The brontosaur Bonds gave him the key to Earth before he died."

"That must be why they are keeping his mother alive in here. They must know he has it."

"How is she doing?"

"Her leg is broken, but I put a splint on it. She should be alright."

"Let me tell Prodie and Yiddah what's going on. Prodie won't stop scratching my leg. Oh, and tell Yiddah's mother that her son is here with us. I'll be right back."

"Okay."

Tuck opened his eyes and looked down at Prodie.

Prodie got up and put his front paws on Tuck's knees, searching his eyes. "Well?" He demanded. "Is Noelle alright?"

Tuck hesitated a moment, reaching out his hand, stroking Prodie on the head.

"Is she dead?" Prodie whimpered.

"We don't know," Tuck said. "She was trying to escape to warn us, but she was caught by a wolf. I'm sure that she will be fine," he said, reassuring himself as much as Prodie.

"I know that she is fine," Prodie announced. "We need to kick some tyrannosaur butt and get her back," he growled, squashing a bug with his paw.

"Tough little blighter," Yiddah smiled. "Glad you are on our side," he added, giving the beagle a pat on the head.

"By the way," Tuck said to Yiddah, "Your mother is with Sienne. Her leg is possibly broken, but Sienne has cleaned and mended it."

"Thank you," Yiddah said with sincerity.

*   *   *

"Your son is on his way here with my friends to get us out," Sienne told Yenzl.

"But it is too dangerous!" Yenzl exclaimed. "And, how do you know this?" She added, raising an eyebrow.

"I have been communicating with my friend Tuck with my mind," Sienne answered. "Long story," she added quickly, to stop any questions. "Let me talk some more with my friend to figure a way out of here."

She closed her eyes. "Tuck, are you there?"

"Hang on," Tuck said to Prodie and Yiddah. "Sienne's back."

"I'm here," Tuck answered. "How is your leg? I saw you limping when the T-rexes took you."

"It's a little bruised still, but it won't slow me down," she answered, flexing her ankle.

"So, what's the plan?" She asked.

"We don't have one yet," he answered. "We should be near the T-rexes' lair by late afternoon."

Tuck hesitated. "Are you sure it was a wolf that caught Noelle?" He asked.

"I'm pretty sure. Why? You don't think," Sienne started as it dawned on her where Tuck was going with his question.

"Yes, I think it must be the wolf that Sentra was telling us about," Tuck interrupted. "The one with the ability to jump to the dinosaur sanctuary."

"Then, the stories are true," Sienne gasped. "How do we let Sentra know?"

"I don't think that'll be possible at the moment," Tuck stated. "Anyway, we need to get you out of there and find Noelle. Do you know how many T-rexes we are dealing with?"

"I've only seen the ones that attacked us and their leader, Thorn. He is *huge,* Tuck."

"Well, we have to assume that there are more of them," Tuck said. "Also, not to forget the pterodactyl."

"I only saw one pterodactyl guard when I was bought in," Sienne said.

"All right, then," Tuck exhaled. "We'll talk again when we're closer."

"Okay. Be careful," Sienne said, her voice breaking with worry.

"We will," Tuck answered, and was gone.

Sienne slumped down against the damp wall next to Yenzl, who looked up with large, sad eyes.

"All will be well," Sienne said, stroking the creature's smooth cheek.

Chapter 32

"Well, there it is," Yiddah pointed.

Tuck and Prodie looked up at the castle-like fortress.

"This looks like something from a King Arthur movie," Tuck commented.

"What is a 'King Arthur movie?'" Yiddah asked, frowning.

"King Arthur is a character the humans made up for entertainment using moving pictures which they call a movie," Prodie stated bluntly.

"Okaaay," Yiddah replied hesitantly, looking puzzled.

"How do you know about King Arthur?" Tuck asked, frowning down at the dog.

"I know things," Prodie answered smugly. "I have been watching your tel-e-vision."

"I see," Tuck murmured, giving Prodie a long, hard look.

"I cannot see if any guards are posted," Yiddah said, squinting at the ramparts.

"I'm guessing that's the entrance to their lair," Tuck said, pointing to the staircase. Sienne said she saw only one pterodactyl guard at the stairs."

"That *is* the main entrance," Yiddah confirmed. "This was actually our council structure before the tyrannosaurs killed the brontosaur council members."

"What do you mean by 'main entrance?'" Tuck asked. "Is there another entrance?"

"Do you see the size of those stairs?" Yiddah pointed out. "That is the entrance for the large Dinosaurs. Off to the side is an entrance for us smaller lads," he grinned.

"Do you think the tyrannosaurs know of the other entrance?" Prodie asked.

"I do not think so," Yiddah said. "Since they never had reason to use it. Still, best to be careful. If a wolf is with them, it might know."

"I do not like the look of this," Prodie said, sniffing the air.

"No worries," Yiddah exclaimed, slapping the beagle on the shoulder. "Get the hostages, kill the baddies, and save all the humans from being eaten. Simple," he grinned.

"That's funny," Tuck replied. "It does sum it up, though," he added, thoughtfully.

Prodie's tail relaxed. "Sounds like a plan," he said. "Lead on," he gestured to Yiddah.

"Best we stay close to the base to get to the side entrance," Yiddah said, starting off.

They walked along an almost three-meter-high wall of huge, neatly stacked stones.

"We are near the main entrance," Yiddah announced, bringing the group to a halt. He peered around the corner, his eyes wandering up the stairs into the darkness.

"How does it look?" Tuck whispered.

"Seems to be all clear," Yiddah answered, sounding surprised.

Prodie squeezed his snout between Yiddah and the wall and looked around the corner.

"Watch it, fleabag!" Yiddah said, as he grabbed Prodie by the tail.

"I see nothing moving," Prodie announced, ignoring Yiddah's complaints.

"Shhh!" Tuck said, holding Yiddah's beak shut. "It could be a trap."

"My mar mou molding my mouf mut!" Yiddah complained through Tuck's hand.

Tuck put his finger up to his lips while giving Prodie a stern look. He slowly let go of Yiddah's beak.

"It doesn't make sense that they would pull the guard," Tuck observed.

"Maybe they want us to come through the front door," Prodie said. "Would be easier for them to grab us when we are inside than try and catch us out here."

"Maybe," Tuck said absentmindedly as he surveyed the entrance.

"There!" He hissed. "See the grey wing sticking up from behind that large rock to the left of the entrance?"

Prodie and Yiddah peered around the corner.

"Why is its wing sticking up like that? Is it sleeping?" Prodie wondered out loud.

"I do not think so," Yiddah answered, not taking his eyes off the rock. "You see that small trail of smoke coming from behind the rock? I think the storm must have hit it."

"You could be right," said Tuck. "If the T-rexes haven't noticed that yet, we may have an advantage. They won't be expecting us to come through the front door without the sentry's alarm."

"So, how come you humans call the tyrannosaurs 'T-rexes?'" Yiddah asked, looking up at Tuck with a puzzled look.

"You sure ask some strange questions," Tuck stated as he got down to his knees.

"Well, you humans seem to be a strange lot," Yiddah commented dryly.

"Fair enough," Tuck answered. "We humans officially call them 'Tyrannosaurus Rex,' but we usually just say 'T-rex.'"

"Yeah, you should see all the moving pictures they make up about the tyrannosaurs for entertainment," Prodie eagerly added. "I think they are the humans' favorite baddies."

"Hmm, a little bit different when they are real though, 'eh?" Yiddah remarked.

"So I've been told," Tuck answered, glancing over at Prodie, who was standing nonchalantly with an innocent look on his face.

A low, rumbling growl coming from inside the lair brought them back to reality. They quickly froze, backs against the wall.

"Enough chit chat, I think," Tuck said, his heart beating wildly.

Chapter 33

"So, do we just waltz up to the main entrance?" Prodie asked.

"I don't think so," Tuck replied. "I would have to haul you both up those stairs. I think it best to use the side entrance. We could use a diversion, though."

"How about you go up and roll the pterodactyl down the stairs?" Yiddah started. "That will make a lot of noise and should make them think that we are coming to the rescue. Then, me and Prodie could sneak through the side entrance and get them out."

"That's actually not a bad idea," Tuck said thoughtfully. "Except, I would be up there with no place to go."

They all stared up at the top of stairs deep in thought when a huge figure emerged from the dark blinking its eyes in the bright light.

"Oh, no!" Tuck said through his teeth as they tucked their heads back behind the wall. "Did it see us?"

A loud roar came from the top of the stairs as they heard the tyrannosaur call back into the lair of their presence.

"Yep," said Yiddah. "It did. Follow me, we need to get to the side entrance before they know what we are up too." He peeked around the corner. "Quick, it is still looking back into the lair."

They ran across the opening to the other side of the wall.

At the top of the stairs, all hell was breaking loose. Mauler and Kontch were taking the stairs two at a time with Zahar at their heels. Thorn was bellowing commands.

"Bring them all back alive!" He raged as he stared at the pterodactyl sentry lying sprawled with a black scorch mark on its chest. "Get those two idiots down from the tower," he called to Ka'dilla.

*   *   *

"Up this slope," Yiddah panted.

They clambered up the bushy incline. Tuck grabbed onto vines to haul himself up the incline as his sneakers kept losing grip on the grassy surface. Yiddah and Prodie easily managed the climb with their short-clawed legs.

"Come on!" Yiddah called impatiently, as he and Prodie waited against the castle wall.

"Next time, I'll be sure to be wearing my climbing boots when I have to save the world," Tuck said sarcastically as he leaned, red-faced, against the wall.

"At least you did not have to go up and roll the Pterodactyl down the stairs," Yiddah panted.

"Let's move on, shall we?" Tuck said, glancing at the bottom of the stairs to see the tyrannosaurs looking for them.

They moved gingerly through the prickly underbrush along the wall.

Tuck winced each time a thorn cut into his skin.

"Here it is," Yiddah announced. He spread some bushes aside to reveal a small opening not much larger than a doggie door.

"That will be a tight fit," Tuck said, kneeling down in front of the small opening.

"Oh, you will manage," Yiddah said, patting Tuck's empty belly. "Looks like you have lost some weight lately," he grinned.

"Does sarcasm run in your family?" Tuck asked as he sized up the opening.

Yiddah's head swiveled around. "Someone is coming. We have to hurry," he hissed.

"I will go in first and have a look," Prodie said. "I can see better than you in the dark."

"Okay, go," Tuck said as he squinted over his shoulder through the bushes.

Prodie easily fit through the opening and disappeared.

"Alright," came Prodie's voice from the dark. "You can come through, it is safe."

"I should go next," Tuck said as he heard a voice from below call, "They went this way!"

"Tuck!" Sienne's voice called in his head. "What's going on?"

"Not now, Sienne," he answered. "We are a little busy. Talk to you in a minute."

"Go! Go!" Yiddah said anxiously.

Tuck let out a deep breath as he lay down on his back in front of the opening, stretching his arms into the hole. He wiggled through the opening, first one shoulder, then the other, his fingers feeling along the thickness of the wall. Tuck's fingers walked along about three feet of stone, small spiders scattering as his fingers plowed through their webbing. Finally, his fingers fell onto the inside edge. With his hands, he dragged himself through with Prodie pulling on his shirt collar. Tuck sat up on the inside and pulled his legs through. Yiddah emerged right behind Tuck's shoes.

"Quick, we have to close the opening," Yiddah exclaimed. "I think the wolf is near."

"There is a large rock over here," Prodie said. "Can you lift it?"

Tuck crawled to the rock. "No, it's too heavy," he grunted. "But, I could push it into the opening."

"Hurry!" Yiddah whispered as a shadow fell over the entrance.

Tuck pushed the rock into the entrance just as Zahar's snout sniffed the opening.

The rock filled two-thirds of the opening as Tuck pushed it as far in as he could.

On the outside, Zahar growled as he clawed at the rock.

"They are inside!" He called to the tyrannosaurs.

Tuck slumped breathless against the damp wall.

"How do we find Sienne and Yiddah's mother before the tyrannosaurs get back?" Prodie said.

"I know where they are," came a small voice from the dark.

"Noelle!" Prodie gasped.

Chapter 34

"How did you – we heard you were – what happened to *your tail?*" Prodie panted, licking Noelle lovingly on the cheek and then eyeing her now-stumpy tail.

"We do not have time to chat," she said anxiously, trying to dodge the long, flapping tongue.

"Where's Sienne?" Tuck asked, kneeling in front of Noelle, his eyes finally having adjusted to the dark interior.

"I will take you to her," she answered. "And to Yenzl," she added, looking at Yiddah.

"One of the tyrannosaurs has gone up the tower to get the other two," she whispered, pointing to an entrance at the opposite end of the Lair.

"And there are at least three tyrannosaurs and a wolf coming up the main entrance," hissed Yiddah.

"Looks like we'll be boxed in here," Tuck stated. "Let's get Sienne and Yenzl. Maybe we can make it back to this small entrance before they get here," he said, his voice belying his uncertainty.

"This way," Noelle said as she started off.

The pitter-patter of paws and shoes echoed off the glistening walls.

"In here," Noelle motioned.

"Sienne!" Tuck called into the dark.

"Tuck?" Sienne answered. "Tuck, be careful! There's a drop-off."

"I see it," he answered.

Tuck lay on his stomach and stretched his arms downwards. "Pass Yiddah's mother up," he said.

Sienne gently picked up Yenzl. "Time to go," she said, lifting her up to Tuck's outstretched arms. "Be careful, her leg..."

"I know. I have her."

"Oh, my," Yenzl said, eyes darting nervously about as Tuck gently hoisted her over the ledge.

"Mother!" Yiddah cried in relief. "Are you alright?" He said, hugging her tightly.

"I will be fine," she said, calmly patting Yiddah on the back. "A nice female human helped me."

"Pull harder!" Sienne called.

With one huge effort, Tuck pulled Sienne up over the ledge. They both fell into a crumpled heap. They lay there for a breathless moment.

"We need to go *now!*" Prodie exclaimed, looking nervously towards the main entrance.

Angry roars where making their way down towards them from the main entrance.

"Let's get out of here," Tuck exclaimed. "Yiddah, I'll carry your mom," he said, gently picking up Yenzl.

"All will be well, Mother," Yiddah said.

"I know, Dear," Yenzl cooed.

Tuck cradled Yenzl in his left arm as they moved swiftly towards the small entrance.

"Are you comfortable enough?" Tuck asked.

"Yes, thank you," Yenzl replied evenly.

"Oh-oh," Prodie barked, as three tyrannosaurs emerged from the tower staircase.

"Get them!" Bellowed Ka'Dilla.

Thrill and Seeker roared, as they lowered their heads and charged.

"Wait!" Tuck said, halting the group and looking back. "We're not going to make it."

The wolf and three tyrannosaurs came bounding towards them. He looked up and saw light coming from a small barred window. A tiny creature was perched on the ledge. "Sonki?" Tuck thought to himself.

"Tuck!" Noelle squeaked, her voice quaking with fear.

"It's okay," Tuck answered, bending to put Yenzl down and giving Noelle a reassuring stroke on the cheek. "I have a plan."

"Everyone stay close," he said, laying his hands on Yiddah and Prodie. "We have to conjure up the dome," he said to Sienne who looking at him curiously through widened eyes.

"You know what you're doing?" She asked, noticing the calmness in his eyes.

"It will be alright," he said, taking her hands in his.

"Hurry!" Prodie cried as the lumbering tyrannosaurs followed by the wolf closed in on them.

Tuck and Sienne raised their arms. The barely-visible dome fell over their heads.

The tyrannosaur Thrill was the first to come, crashing headfirst into the dome, jarring Tuck and Sienne's arms.

Thrill fell into an unconscious heap, blood oozing from his putrid mouth.

"Wait!" Zahar yelped, as the other tyrannosaurs began head-butting the dome.

Zahar and Thorn began arguing, their muffled voices barely audible inside the dome.

"Prodie," Tuck said carefully. "See if you can penetrate the dome."

Prodie gave an anxious whimper as he eyed the circling tyrannosaurs.

"Just try and stick a paw through," Tuck hissed anxiously, his arms beginning to shake.

Prodie gingerly raised a paw towards the wall of the dome. It went through with no resistance. Prodie quickly pulled it back in.

"Good," Tuck said, eying Zahar, who was watching him intently. The tyrannosaurs had taken up positions around the dome and were watching and waiting.

"I will see that Thorn eats you," Tuck thought as he stared into the wolf's eyes.

Zahar blinked and took a tentative step back.

Tuck smiled.

"He heard you," Sienne gasped, sweat running down her face.

Zahar recovered quickly. "You will not get out of here, human," Zahar's voice appeared in Tuck's head.

"We shall see," Tuck answered, gazing into Zahar's eyes.

Tuck smiled again and turned to look at Seeker.

"Get the wolf!" Came a voice inside Seeker's mind. "It is going to double-cross us all."

Seeker's hulking head spun to look at Zahar.

Zahar looked first at Seeker and then back to Tuck. As it dawned on him what was happening, he narrowed his eyes and flared his yellowing teeth.

"The wolf is going to double-cross us!" Seeker roared as he charged at Zahar.

"What?" Thorn yelled in disbelief as Seeker rounded on Zahar.

"Idiot!" Zahar spat, crouching against the floor, ready to leap. "The human is putting words in his head!"

"What?" Thorn repeated, watching Seeker barrel past Mauler and Kontch.

"Prodie, Noelle," Tuck cried. "Go now! Get to the main entrance!"

"But – " Noelle hesitated.

"Go. We'll be alright," he said, gesturing with his chin.

They stared at Tuck for a moment, looked at one another, turned and ran straight through the dome wall.

"Stop the buffoon!" Cried Zahar as Seeker bared down on him. "He is being controlled by the human."

Thorn stepped in front of Zahar and lowered his huge head, knocking the charging tyrannosaur off his feet. Seeker flew backwards through the air and landed with a loud thud on the cobble-stone floor. He did not get up.

Thorn turned on Zahar. "What do you mean, the human is controlling him?"

"Where are the other two?" Zahar yelled, ignoring the question and peering into the dome.

"Two down, five to go," Tuck's voice came mockingly into Zahar's mind.

When Zahar's eyes met Tuck's, Tuck could detect the first traces of fear.

"Find them!" Thorn thundered.

Mauler and Kontch thumped off in pursuit.

"Which way did they go?" Kontch asked in a loud whisper.

"I don't know," answered Mauler angrily. "Let's just pretend we know," he said as they headed towards the tower.

"And then there were three," came a calm voice in Zahar's mind.

"Tuck!" Sienne called. "I can't hold this much longer."

"Just hang in there one more minute," Tuck said, meeting her pained eyes.

Sienne arms were shaking uncontrollably.

This time, when Tuck looked back at Zahar, the wolf was smiling.

Chapter 35

"Do you still have the key?" Tuck asked Yiddah.

Yiddah gave Tuck a quizzical look, head slightly tilted.

"The key Bonds gave you," Tuck hissed, sweat dripping from his nose.

"Oh, the key! Yes," Yiddah said. He reached into a fold of skin to reveal the disc. A ray of sunlight caught it, and a spectacular blue-green light flashed about the dirty walls.

"Good," Tuck said. "When I give the word, I want you to throw it up as high as you can."

"You want to just give the key to Earth to *them?*" Queried Yiddah, pointing at the tyrannosaurs.

"Yiddah, there's no time. We can't keep the dome up any longer."

"On with it then," Yiddah quipped.

Tuck looked up at Sonki on the ledge. "Ready?" He thought.

Sonki nodded.

Sienne looked from Sonki to Tuck. "I hope this works," she said. Her whole body was shaking from the effort.

"The compi has the key to Earth!" Thorn exclaimed, mesmerized by the flashing blue and green.

They watched as Yiddah pulled his arm back. Like a slingshot, he flung his arm forward, releasing the key.

The shimmering disc pierced through the dome's wall and arched high into the air.

The heads of Thorn, Ka'Dilla, Tusker and Zahar all followed its path.

Zahar swore under his breath as he turned back just in time to see Tuck, Sienne and the compi running for the main entrance. "I will get you later," Zahar scowled as he looked back to see the key being snatched in Thorn's huge mouth.

From the small window, Sonki glided down and landed on Thorns head. "Earth," she said.

Zahar, Tusker and Ka'Dilla stared in amazement as a gateway opened up in front of Thorn. A deep blue light lit up the lair as the opening rapidly increased. Thorn looked at Ka'Dilla, horror in his eyes as he and Sonki toppled through the opening and disappeared.

"Where did he go?" Ka'Dilla said hysterically, looking about.

Zahar didn't bother answering. He turned and ran after the others.

"Where are you going, wolf?" Ka'Dilla called after him. *"Get him!"* She shrieked at Tusker.

*　　　*　　　*

Tuck placed Yenzl gently on the ground. "Is anyone coming?" He asked.

Sienne peeked around the wall. "No," she panted. Then, she ducked. "Wait, the wolf is at the top of the stairs."

Zahar narrowed his eyes at the place where Sienne's head disappeared. He bounded down the stairs, threads of drool lashing his face as the anger raged inside him. He rounded the wall snarling, teeth bared. His jaw dropped as he absorbed the sight before him.

Behind Tuck and the others stood Sentra before a hoard of twenty massive dinosaurs – a mixture of triceratops and brontosaurs. His brain recovered quickly. Zahar's front legs dug into the ground as his hind legs began to back peddle. The triceratops snorted and pawed the ground, impatiently waiting for the order to charge. In one smooth motion, Zahar spun around, his tail swishing past Tuck's face. As a small hole began to open in front of Zahar, he started to leap through the widening gateway.

"No!" Yelled Tuck. He lunged forward, grabbing the wolf's tail.

"Wait!" Cried Prodie. He sunk his teeth onto Tuck's jean's cuff. All three were pulled through the opening.

Zahar hit the ground on all fours. Shaking Tuck off his tail, he immediately headed for a line of trees.

"Uff!" Tuck grunted as he and Prodie landed face first onto the dry dusty surface.

"Did you see which way he went?" Tuck asked, sitting up and spitting dust from his mouth.

"Towards that wooded area," Prodie answered, a cloud of dust rising as he violently shook his compact body.

"You shouldn't have come," Tuck said. "But, I'm glad you did," he said with a smile.

"You would be lost without me," Prodie said, smiling. "You are on *my* sanctuary now," he added, looking around.

"You know where we are, then," Tuck said, standing up and brushing the dust off his stained shirt.

"Our council structure is over those hills to the west, about two day's walk," Prodie gestured.

Prodie surveyed the area around them. "Hmmm," he murmured, frowning.

"I don't like the sound of that 'hmmm,'" Tuck said, looking in the direction Prodie was looking.

"Those trees where the wolf disappeared into," he started. "That's where . . ."

"Wait!" Tuck exclaimed.

"Come and get me, human," Zahar's voice hissed in Tuck's mind.

"What is it?" Asked Prodie.

"It's the wolf. It wants us to come after him."

"I am waiting," Zahar voice said mockingly.

"He isn't far away," Tuck said. "I can sense him."

"I think we should go back and get help," Prodie said, nervously eyeing the tree line.

"No," Tuck said, staring at the woods. "It ends here."

"This way," he said, Zahar's taunting whispers cutting through his thoughts.

Prodie sniffed the ground as they swiftly moved into the dense woods.

"Hang on!" Tuck hissed, his mind straining. "I can't sense him anymore."

Tuck and Prodie moved slowly into a clearing, all their senses on edge.

"Show yourself, wolf," Tuck whispered, as he moved to the edge of a ravine.

"Do not get too close," warned Prodie. "That is a bottomless p – Tuck, watch out!" Prodie screamed. "The wolf!"

Zahar came bounding silently out of the woods towards Tuck.

Tuck spun around to see Prodie charging head first into Zahar's hindquarters as he leapt, knocking Zahar's body sideways in the air. Tuck ducked as the wolf sailed over his head. Zahar twisted his body in mid-air and with one paw managed to latch onto Tuck's shirt collar.

Tuck yelled with surprise as he was yanked off his feet.

Prodie watched in horror as both Tuck and the wolf disappeared over the edge into the ravine.

"Tuck!" Prodie screamed. He ran to look over the edge, dreading the sight of Tuck tumbling into the deep black ravine. There was only Zahar's cloak to be seen, floating lazily down into the darkness. Prodie lifted his head and howled, his eyes filling with tears.

"Instead of sitting there and howling, how's about giving me a hand?" Came a voice from directly below the dog.

"Arrrroooo – what?" Prodie said, in mid howl, looking about for where the voice came from.

"Down here," came Tuck's voice.

Tuck saw Prodie's quivering snout appear over the edge. "Tuck!" He shouted, tail wagging excitedly. Tuck was hanging from a short thick root that was sticking out just below the edge.

"Is there anything I can grab onto up there?" He asked.

Prodie looked about. "Yes, about two feet from your left, there is a thick root just above the ground right near the edge. Looks pretty sturdy," he said, eyes sparkling with happiness.

"Okay," Tuck said letting out a breath of air. "I can't see it. I'll have to swing myself and let go with one hand and make a grab for the root. You're absolutely positive it's where you say it is?"

Prodie disappeared for a moment. "Yes," he said when he reappeared.

"Alright, here goes," Tuck said, swinging his body to the side until he had enough momentum. He let go with his left hand as his body swung up and grabbed for the root.

"Got it," he said as his right hand appeared next to his left hand. He pulled himself up with Prodie pulling on the already-ripped collar. Tuck slumped onto his back breathing heavily as Prodie began licking his face with happiness.

*   *   *

Earth, South Pacific Ocean.

Thorn's flailing body splashed into the water. A moment later, he surfaced, kicking to stay afloat, Sonki hovering above him. Thorn stared at Sonki, hatred and horror flashed across his eyes as he opened his jaws. "Hom – gahg!" He coughed and slipped below the surface. Sonki circled until the waters were calm once more.

"Home," she whispered. She stared one last time at the place where Thorn had gone under, satisfied that he was really gone, flew through the gateway, and disappeared.

Chapter 36

"Tuck!" Sienne cried as he and Prodie stepped out of thin air practically in front of the group. She and Noelle ran over to meet them. Sienne hugged Tuck tightly.

"It's over," he said, holding her and patting her on the back.

Noelle and Prodie nuzzled each other's necks.

"Do not ever take off like that again," she scolded, eyes filling with tears.

"All good," he panted, relieved.

He and Tuck looked at each other and smiled.

"So," piped in Sentra. "I am glad to see you are both safe."

Tuck took Sienne's hand and walked up to Sentra.

"How did you manage to make it back here without Sienne?" Sentra asked curiously.

Sienne and Tuck smiled at each other.

"With telepathy," Tuck answered. "We thought of the same place to jump too and it worked," he added, smiling again.

"And the wolf?" Sentra asked.

"Into a bottomless pit," Tuck said.

"Hmmm."

Tuck turned to the sound of deep grumbles just in time to see Tusker, Ka 'Dilla and Thrill being led off by two brontosaurs and four triceratops.

"What happened to the other T-rex?" Tuck queried, noticing one missing.

"The one called Seeker was found dead in the lair," replied Sentra.

"What will happen to them?" Asked Sienne, eying the dinosaurs as they trudged by.

"They will be separated and put to work under close supervision."

"You have done well," Sentra commended, laying her outstretched wings on their shoulders.

114

"Hey," Prodie called up to her, looking hurt.

"Nothing would have been possible without you two," Tuck said, bending down as he and Sienne picked up Prodie and Noelle.

"Indeed," Sentra smiled, cupping them both under the chin with her wingtips.

"Where's Yiddah?" Tuck said, looking about.

"He is over there by the bushes with the rest of his family," Sentra pointed.

Yiddah looked up to see them looking his way. He gave a ceremonial bow of gratitude. Tuck smiled and nodded as Yenzl gave a cheery wave, Sienne waved back, a tear rolled down her cheek.

"Their clan has lost a couple of its members to a tyrannosaur attack," Sentra stated. "Give them some time to mourn, we will all get together soon."

"We most definitely will," Tuck said, absentmindedly scratching Prodie under the chin.

"Is Sonki here?" Sienne asked.

"She is waiting for us on bird sanctuary," Sentra answered.

"And Thorn?" Tuck asked.

"At the bottom of the Pacific ocean," she replied.

Sentra tilted her head slightly as she looked at Tuck. "You will have to tell me how you managed to send Thorn through the gate to Earth – but let us go to bird sanctuary," she quickly added. "I have tea waiting with Sonki and Ceril."

"Ceril," Sienne said, concerned. "How is he?"

Sentra smiled. "He is just fine. Shall we go?"

Tuck gave one look back as the last of the triceratops trudged by.

Tuck and Sienne put their hand on Sentra as she murmured, "Home."

A gateway opened up. They stepped through and disappeared.

Chapter 37

"About time you all showed up," Ceril snorted as Tuck and Sienne, holding Prodie and Noelle, appeared with Sentra. Ceril and Sonki were standing on a short fat stump in the picnic area. Ceril's feet were dancing a nervous jig with excitement.

"How are you doing, you ol' buzzard?" Tuck said, smiling as he lowered Prodie to the ground and began ruffling Ceril's feathered head.

"Old buzzard!" Ceril spluttered.

"Ceril," Sienne cooed. "I'm glad you're okay. How's the wing?"

"It will mend," he replied, gingerly flexing his injured wing. "Just have to hop around for a few days."

"Our turn," Prodie grumbled.

"Hey!" Ceril said excitedly, as he hopped off the stump to greet them.

Sienne looked at Sonki, who was standing quietly on the stump.

"You were amazing," she said, leaning over and giving her a kiss on the cheek.

Tuck and Sonki looked at each other, smiling.

"How did you manage to get back on bird sanctuary?" Sienne asked.

"Soon after the storm passed, someone from Yiddah's clan came for us," she explained. "We went to bird sanctuary with Yiddah's father, Yalpus, to have Ceril tended to, and Sentra and I came back with Yalpus."

"And a good thing you did too," Tuck commented. "We'll also have to thank Eejh for getting the message to Yiddah's clan," he added.

"So, Tuck," Sentra started, "It seems that you are able to use telepathy to communicate with others."

"So it would seem," he replied.

"Sonki was telling me about how she could hear your voice in her mind," she said.

"Well, I saw that we had basically no chance of escaping from the lair, what with all the T-rexes closing in from all sides," he said. "I then sensed Sonki and saw her up on the ledge. The plan just hit me. Once Yiddah threw the disc in the air, Sonki would come down and land on Thorn and send him through the gateway to Earth, where he would hopefully not be found again."

"I am impressed," Sentra acknowledged.

"Well, there was also a bit of luck involved," he said. "I was counting on Thorn catching the key and not one of the others, or there may have been a much different ending."

"Well, it all worked out as it should have," Sentra concluded. "Tea anyone?" She asked as seven white cranes gracefully landed, each placing a wooden flecked bowl of steaming tea onto the stumps. The cranes bowed, turned and kicked off into the air, their wings whooshing quietly as they gained height.

"I took the liberty of choosing the tea," Sentra said. "I hope you will be happy with my choice."

Prodie walked up and sniffed one of the two bowls that Tuck placed on the ground for him and Noelle.

"Chinese Cherry with a hint of ginger and honey," Sentra announced.

"Not bad," Prodie said, lapping at his tea. "Still, it could use a nice juicy bone," he mumbled.

"Prodie!" Noelle scolded as the others laughed.

"Don't worry, my friend," Tuck said, sitting cross-legged on the ground next to Prodie. "When we get back home, I'll get you the biggest bone I can find," he smiled.

Prodie stopped lapping his tea and looked up at Sentra. Tuck's smile disappeared as he noticed the seriousness on Prodie's face. He looked back from Sentra to Prodie.

"Are Prodie and Noelle not coming back to Earth with us?" Sienne asked, worry suddenly enveloping her face.

"That will be entirely up to them," Sentra said after a brief thought.

Tuck and Sienne looked at Prodie and Noelle.

"You don't want to come back with us?" Tuck asked, staring into Prodie's chocolate eyes.

Prodie stared back at Tuck for what seemed an eternity. "Of course we are coming back with you," he finally blurted out. "Somebody has to watch over you."

"You little rat-bag," Tuck said as he grabbed Prodie and rolled him onto his back and began giving him a belly rub. Prodie moaned with delight as the others began laughing.

As the white cranes flew off with the empty teacups, Tuck, Sienne, Prodie and Noelle began saying their goodbyes.

"You will, of course, be coming back for the celebration feast to be held in your honor," Sentra said.

"We wouldn't miss it for the world," Sienne said, taking Sentra's wing.

"I guess we'll be seeing you two up in some tree somewhere," Tuck said, stroking Sonki and Ceril along their backs.

"Oh, we will be around alright," Ceril said, matter-of-factly.

"All right, then," he smiled. "Let's go, shall we?" He said to Sienne as he picked up Prodie.

"Do not forget your sweatshirt," Sonki called after them. Tuck turned as Sonki landed onto his shoulder with his sweatshirt in her beak.

"Thanks," he said as they looked deep into each other's eyes, silence bonding their friendship. Sonki flew back onto the stump with Ceril as Tuck put Prodie down and pulled the sweatshirt over his dusty ripped shirt.

"That looks a bit better," Sienne said, looking him up and down.

"Ready?" Tuck asked.

"Ummm . . . Noelle," Sienne began. "Didn't you say something about that we wouldn't have to worry about time. It has been almost two days. We'll have been missed at home by now."

"Of course," Noelle exclaimed. "I almost forgot. You both only have to envision the time and place where you left and we will be sent back there."

"Sounds simple enough," Tuck said.

"Remember," Sentra began, "You *both* have to envision the same time and place, or you will be separated and be placed in different times.

"So, I know it was Tuesday," Tuck said. "About half-past-two in the afternoon, right?"

"Closer to 3:00 pm, I think," Sienne said. "Mom had just taken the cookies out of the oven, and that was 2:45 pm."

"Okay," Tuck said, relieved. "Three o'clock on Friday the 28th of December in your dad's study."

Sienne thought a moment. "Sounds about right," she agreed.

They turned and gave one last wave to Sentra, Sonki and Ceril. Tuck and Sienne closed their eyes and murmured, "home."

A gateway opened in front of them, growing rapidly in size as the furnishings of the study came in view. Tuck and Sienne stepped through and were gone.

Chapter 38

"The coast is clear," Sienne whispered as she peered down the hallway.

"We'll be right back," Tuck said to Prodie and Noelle as he and Sienne slipped into the bathroom across the hallway.

"God, I look a fright," Sienne said, starting as she saw herself in the mirror.

Tuck splashed water onto his face and run his wet hands through his hair. "That will have to do," he said to his reflection.

Sienne grunted and swore as she forced a brush through her thick, mangled hair. Tuck peeked out the doorway as Sienne took a sweater out of the laundry hamper and pulled it over her stained shirt.

"Not much better," Prodie said as they returned.

"As soon as we get home, I'll be taking a long bath," Tuck stated.

"So," Sienne began, "I, um, we'll see you both tomorrow, then," she said glancing at Prodie.

"You can count on that," Prodie said, touching noses with Noelle.

They all walked silently towards the door.

"Leaving so soon?" Mrs. McCally asked.

"Um, yes," Tuck answered, turning to his side so Sienne's mother would not notice the torn jeans. "I still have some chores to do," he fibbed.

"Hope to see you again soon," she said as she walked back into the kitchen.

"Bye," he said.

Sienne opened the door. The cold hit them like a wave.

"I'd forgotten that it's winter," Tuck said as he felt the goose bumps rising on his arms.

Tuck and Sienne gazed at each other silently. "So, how closely related *are* we, do you think?" Tuck asked, taking Sienne's hand in his.

Sienne thought a moment. "I don't know," she pondered. "We'll have to ask Sentra about that." She gave Tuck a quick hug.

"Looks like times will be good," Prodie said, as he nuzzled Noelle's neck.

"Indeed," she said, eyes closed.

"We'll come by around 10 tomorrow and we can do something," Tuck said as he and Prodie walked out the door.

"Sounds good," Sienne replied.

"See you tomorrow, Noelle," Tuck said.

"See you tomorrow."

Sienne closed the door.

*　　　*　　　*

Zahar moaned as he attempted to move.

"Do not try to move, wolf," came a high-pitched voice. "You are injured."

"Where am I?" He groaned. "How did I get here?"

"I summoned you," the voice said.

Zahar opened his eyes a sliver. A long pointy black snout with quivering whiskers came slowly into focus.

"Who . . . who are you?" He croaked just as his eyes fell shut again, and darkness fell over him like a blanket as he slipped back into unconsciousness.

Lightning Source UK Ltd.
Milton Keynes UK
UKOW05f2203141013

219063UK00002B/527/P